Swallowing Mercury

Wioletta Greg

Translated from the Polish by Eliza Marciniak

BOOKS

Published by Portobello Books in 2017

Portobello Books
12 Addison Avenue
London
W11 4QR

This book has been selected to receive financial assistance from English PEN's
PEN Translates programme, supported by Arts Council England. English
PEN exists to promote literature and our understanding of it, to uphold
writers' freedoms around the world, to campaign against the persecution and
imprisonment of writers for stating their views, and to promote the friendly
cooperation of writers and the free exchange of ideas. www.englishpen.org

Supported using public funding by
**ARTS COUNCIL
ENGLAND**

A CIP catalogue record for this book is available from the British Library

9 8 7 6 5 4 3 2 1

ISBN 978 1 84627 607 1
eISBN 978 1 84627 608 8

www.portobellobooks.com

Typeset in Galliard by Patty Rennie
Printed and bound by CPI Group (UK) Ltd Croydon, CRO 4YY

MIX
Paper from
responsible sources
FSC
www.fsc.org FSC® C020471

Contents

The Fairground Girl	1
The Jesus Raffle	6
Little Table, Set Thyself!	15
Waiting for the Popemobile	22
The Little Paint Girl	28
A Picture Pays a Visit	40
Whitsunday	45
An Easter Pasha	49
Spiders from Jerusalem	57
Waves	61
Gienek the Combine Driver	65
Pierced Lids	70
The Dressmaker's Secret	74
Strawberry	79
The Woman with a Dog	85
Sour Cherries	90
The Phillumenist	95

Dolce Vita   102

Masters of Scrap   107

The Return of Zorro   118

The Belated Feeding of Bees   123

Unripe   128

Neon over the Jupiter   137

Translator's Note   143

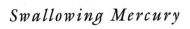

Swallowing Mercury

The Fairground Girl

A CHRISTENING SHAWL DECORATED WITH periwinkle and yellowed asparagus fern hung in the window of our stone house for nearly two years. It tempted me with a little rose tucked in its folds, and I would have used it as a blanket for my dolls, but my mother wouldn't let me go near it.

'Don't touch the shawl, Loletka. It's a memento. We'll take it down when your dad comes back,' she'd say. And when her friend who lived nearby would pop in 'for a moment' – meaning two hours – she would repeat the story of how, a month after my father was arrested for deserting from the army and two weeks before her baby was due, she received a summons to start a work placement at Cem-Build. Together with a dozen other women, she had to make paving slabs as part of the new five-year plan, so that the district government could create new squares in front of office buildings, schools and health centres within the allotted time. In the end, Mum couldn't take working outside in the freezing weather. She hid behind a cement mixer, and when her waters broke into a bucket full of lime they drove her to the maternity ward.

She brought me home in February. Still bleeding after childbirth, she lay down on the bed, unwrapped my blanket, which reeked of mucus and urine, rubbed the stump of my umbilical cord with gentian violet, tied a red ribbon around my wrist to ward off evil spells and fell asleep for a few hours. It was the sort of sleep during which a person decides whether to depart or to turn back.

Dad remained absent. His letters, decorated with drawings of plants and animals, kept accumulating in a shoebox while the pages of the calendar kept falling away, until only a thin stack of days separated us from the end of the year. A few more months passed. Ducklings hatched in the hallway, and Mum moved them with their mother to the pigsty, where they were close to the water-filled piece of tyre in the yard. My grandfather started to plane down new window shutters for the attic and rockers for my rocking horse. My grandmother made colourful cockerels from strips of aspen bast. The flies living between the window frames reawakened. When the christening shawl had faded and the periwinkle leaves had fallen onto the windowsill, a thin man with curly hair and a little moustache came into our house. After he saw me, he cried for a whole day, and he calmed down only when Poland started playing in the World Cup.

In June, we went to the parish fair at St Anthony's Basilica. The procession began. The priest came out of the church, followed by embroidered banners and women dressed up as princesses carrying plaited straw lambs and wreaths. Girls who had recently received First Communion scattered lupin flowers under their feet. I was mesmerised, and when Mum started searching through her bag for coins for the collection tray, I let go of her hand and ran after the procession as if it were a royal entourage. I didn't stop until I reached a market stall with a blown-up silver whale. The whale wasn't able to float off towards the clouds. The sun caught it in red and purple rings and blinded me, burning my cheeks. Gilt figures kept disappearing between the cars and the britchkas, leaving elongated shadows on a wall.

A balding llama was standing under a tree, drooling. People would come up to it, throw money into a tin chained to the fence and mount their children on the animal's back, which was covered with a patterned blanket, while a man in a straw hat would snap photos with a clever camera that spat out prints instantly. The llama gazed sadly from under its long lashes. Little burnt flashbulbs were spinning in its eyes. I wanted to pet its matted forelock, but just at that moment a toy cap gun went off. The frightened llama jumped, and I hid under the plastic tablecloth of the nearest stall. Outside, wrappers were rustling; trumpets, whistles, wind-up toys and harmonicas were playing. I covered my ears and sat under the stall while raspberry juice dripped from the plastic tablecloth right onto my new dress.

Wasps began circling around my plaits like striped piranhas, drinking juice from the little roses on the fabric of my dress and growing larger and larger. One nasty wasp sat on my head, buzzing behind my ear. I lay down on the dry ground and cried out, 'Mummy! Mummy! The wasps want to kidnap me!' But Mum wasn't there.

The plastic tablecloth was drawn aside, and I saw the Moustache Man. 'That's where you are! My... my...' He pulled me out from under the stall and hugged me close. 'My little fairground girl! Where have you been?! I've been looking for you everywhere.'

'Lemme go, Daddy, lemme go!' I squeaked merrily and secretly wiped my snotty nose on his lapel. The Moustache Man, probably delighted that I had called him Daddy for the first time, lifted me up and spun me around in the air. I half-closed my eyes and burst out laughing. The sun's rays pierced the wasps, which shrank back to their normal size and flew off through the red and purple rings. The light tickled me like water during a bath in the wooden washtub in our yard. I felt hungry and started chewing on the edge of my belt. Mum leaned out from the dark alcove of the bus shelter, her head wreathed with a string of little bagels.

The Jesus Raffle

DISOBEYING MY MOTHER, I STARTED SLEEPING with Blacky. Blacky smelled of hay and milk and had a snow white map of Africa around his neck. He would come to me in the night, lie on my duvet and start purring, kneading the covers like dough under his paws. Ever since I found him up in the attic, we lived in a strange state of symbiosis. I'd carry him inside my jumper like a baby, steal cream for him from the dresser and, on Sundays, feed him chicken wings from my soup.

I spent the whole summer roaming the fields with Blacky. He showed me a different kind of geometry of the world, where boundaries are not marked by field margins overgrown with thistles and goosefoot, by cobbled roads, fences or tracks trodden by humans, but instead by light, sound and the elements. With Blacky, I learned to climb haystacks, apple and cherry trees, piles of breeze blocks; I learned to keep away from limestone pits hidden by blackberry bushes, from hornets' nests, quagmires and snares set in the grain fields.

After Christmas, Blacky began to avoid me. He'd turn up at home only briefly and deposit a dead mouse on the doorstep, as if he wanted to make amends for his absence. On the first day of the winter break, he disappeared for good. I searched for him under tarpaulins and in the empty boxes where Uncle Lolek used to breed coypus and where Blacky loved sleeping all day, but he was nowhere to be found.

Uncle Lolek was my main suspect in the case of Blacky's disappearance. A few months earlier, he had somehow managed to get hold of a sack of sugar which he hid in the coal shed, and that's exactly where Blacky set up his litter box. So, armed with my father's air rifle, I ran to confront Uncle Lolek. I pointed the gun at him and ordered him to hand over Blacky immediately, since I couldn't allow my kitty to be turned into sausages and fur, like those nasty-smelling coypus. Uncle Lolek was speechless, and then he burst out laughing so hard he almost fell into the sauerkraut barrel. Grateful for being cheered up so much first thing in the morning, he offered me some sweets.

At dawn the next day, I struck up a conversation with the milkman, who had stopped his horse at the bottom of our dirt drive and was pulling milk churns up onto his cart with a big hook.

'Excuse me, have you seen Blacky?'

'Who?'

'My black cat.'

'Bah!' he spat. 'That's all I need, some black mouser crossing my path today! Mind you, there was some spotty thing hanging round the bridge.'

'No, not a tabby cat… But if you see a black one, can you please let me know?'

'Ah, wait, Wiolitka, I've got something for you.' He gave me a packet of vanilla cream cheese from the co-op, urged his horse forward and drove off.

I wandered around Hektary for a couple more hours, looking in drainpipes and clumps of willow bushes. Finally, I went home, chilled to the bone. My father had come back from work and was sitting on the sofa, soaking his frozen feet in warm salted water and carving a fishing float out of polyfoam. Quietly, so that he wouldn't notice me, I climbed the ladder up to the attic, buried myself in hay and tried to find some trace of Blacky: a scrap of fur, a feather, an eggshell.

'What are you doing up there in this chill?' my father called.

'I'm waiting for Blacky, Dad. He's been missing for three days now.'

'Come down, or you'll freeze. We can bake some potatoes in the ash pan if you want.'

'I'm not coming down until Blacky is back.'

'Come on, get down. I know what's happened.'

I came down the ladder so fast it felt like I was flying. I was lucky that a sack of oats had been propped up against the lowest rungs, or I would have knocked out the last of my milk teeth as I fell. I sat down in the corner by the Christmas tree, nervously crumpling dry spruce needles as I waited for the news, but my father was silent. He finished painting the last bright yellow stripe on the float, put it on top of the *People's Tribune* by the stove and sat down across from me.

'Well... How should I say this...' he began. 'Three days ago, Blacky tried to pull a fish head out of a muskrat snare and he drowned in the pond,' he said in one breath and looked at me anxiously.

I lay down on the sofa and turned to face the straw mat on the wall. For the next week, I didn't speak to anyone; I only whispered to myself. There was nothing strange in that, really, since everyone in our house was always whispering or singing something under their breath. For example, my grandmother would recite the Litany of the Blessed Virgin Mary as she prepared little round dumplings for soup; 'Mother Somethingorother,'

9

repeated the walls and the glass hen for storing eggs; 'Mother Somethingorother,' repeated the embroidered wall hangings, the mirrors, the springs sticking out of the sofa propped on its four birch pegs. My father would hum Elvis songs and prison ballads, such as 'Black Bread and Black Coffee', improvising on a lime-tree leaf or a banjo; my mother would sing 'A Little Bee Sat on an Apple Tree', but only when she was on edge; my grandfather would start his morning in the limestone quarry with the old Resistance song that went, 'On the first of September, Hitler that rogue promised to conquer the world.' But when I muttered or sang to myself, everyone would glance at me with surprise, and Mum would give me more and more drops of the sedative Milocardin on a teaspoon.

One day during the second week of the school break, I sat by the window watering geraniums with cold mint extract. My stomach was hurting because I missed Blacky so much that I had secretly eaten the fringes off the throw on the sofa and some slivers of whitewash from the walls.

My warm breath opened up a gap between the crystal ferns of hoarfrost on the windowpane. I peered out into the yard. An hour later, the front gate creaked, and I could hear my classmates Justyna and Big Witek talking to my mother outside as she emptied the ash pan onto the path. They were wondering if I was coming to St Anthony's Basilica.

'I don't think Wiolka's going with you,' I could hear my mother's hoarse voice. 'She has an upset stomach.'

'But there's going to be a raffle!' Big Witek interrupted her.

'What raffle?'

'Oh, to win a blessed figure,' Justyna explained.

'Then maybe you want to tell her yourselves?'

'They don't have to tell me anything.' I came outside wrapped up to my ears in a woollen shawl. 'I'm going.'

Mum seemed surprised by my sudden recovery but didn't say a word. She poked with her wellies at the patch of warm ashes ringed with glistening brown grass, picked up a sooty nail, threw it on a heap of sand and turned back to the house.

That afternoon, the Łagisza power station had announced on the radio that there would be a period of energy-saving measures. The whole parish had its electricity cut, and the church was as cold as a kennel. The breath of more than a hundred children drifted up in little clouds towards the vault, where fat saints gently floated, as if they were bathing in Lake Balaton. Only a few candles by the altars lit up the nave and the two aisles. The forked light of the setting sun pierced the clay Jesus standing on a pedestal in a light blue robe, with a crown of thorns around his heart. I stood in an aisle, watching a mouse wander around the intricate labyrinth of gilded stucco decorations.

Towards the end, each of us cast a small piece of paper, rubber-stamped by the parish, into a wooden urn. A young girl dressed as an angel drew one out and handed it to the curate. Silence fell. The power came back on. The light blinded us. The hum of the electric fans poured down into the church like a flood. The curate spoke my name. The echo of his voice bounced off the votive offerings. I was so overwhelmed I swallowed my gum, which I had got from Big Witek. The organist intoned 'The Fishing Boat': 'Oh Lord, today Your eyes fell on me. Your lips uttered my name.' The children parted. Justyna pushed me into the middle of the church. I walked slowly in a golden glow all the way to the altar. The curate gave me his stole to kiss, then passed me the statuette of Jesus. Someone grabbed me by the cord of my mittens and led me into the corridor. I went outside accompanied by the children from Hektary, forgetting to dip my fingers in the holy water.

I wrapped the figure up in my woollen shawl, and as night fell Justyna, Big Witek and I took turns carrying it the two and a half miles to Hektary. Small lumps of ice kept falling into our boots. Our hands were frozen stiff, but we paid no attention. We were so excited about our prize that we kept crossing ourselves in front of every roadside shrine and holy spring; Big Witek even crossed himself in front of our headmistress's villa, just in case her Dobermann came running at us through a gap in the fence.

I said goodbye to my friends near the well and ran down our drive to the yard. I paused on the porch and unwrapped the figure. I entered the bright room like a priest making the rounds after Christmas and placed Jesus on the table. It happened to be a feathering evening at our house, and all the women who had come to help my grandmother tear up feathers turned speechless when they saw me. After a pause, they set aside their down-filled farm sieves, kneeled on the floor among the white piles of feathers and started to recite prayers. They didn't have time to say more than two decades of the rosary, however, before their concerned husbands came knocking on our windows.

Late at night, when all the women had gone and I could hear my parents' steady breathing through the partly open door, and after the fire had died down in the stove, I moved the figure to the dining room and put it on a starched napkin, which up to that point had been occupied by our glass hen and a few dead flies. I wrapped myself up in a duvet, since it was terribly cold that February, in 1981, and I stood taut and still in the darkness until the statue rose a little above the napkin. That's when I mustered up the courage to ask Jesus if he could resurrect my Blacky.

Little Table, Set Thyself!

I WOKE UP AT DAWN, REALISING THAT SOMEONE was slinking into the room where I was sleeping. It was my father. In his waterproof cape and wellies, he looked like the mysterious Don Pedro from *The Kidnapping of Balthazar Sponge* cartoons. He cursed the creaky door hinges. Our eyes met in the semi-darkness. He put a finger to his lips, so that I would keep quiet and not alert my mother, but my mother wasn't asleep. She knew what time he got back from fishing on Sundays and was already banging pans around in the kitchen and lighting the fire in the stove. My father undressed, sat down on the sofa, put an immersion heater in a mug and fell asleep instantly. The water danced, sprayed up onto the ceiling and spattered the table, where the blood of the weasel that my father had stuffed the previous week was still clotting in the cracks. A quarter of an hour later, my mother came into the room.

'Rysiek, get up… Come on, get up,' she whispered as he chased a magnificent stag in his dream.

'Mmm…' he muttered. 'If I could stuff it and put it on display on the porch… The whole village would come to see it.'

'Rysiek, the eggs are getting cold. Why did I bother?!'

The raised voice wrenched him out of his dream, but he must have had just enough time to glimpse his wife's golden hair flickering in the undergrowth. She looked like Saint Kunigunde, who had fallen in love with a stag.

'What? How did you get here?' He rubbed his eyes. Between sleep and waking, he seemed to have the impression that pine needles had grown out of his thighs and that brambles had sprung up inside his boots. Strangely, when he woke up, I detected the scent of a forest in the room. He sat up, rocking back and forth over his plate as if he were fishing. 'It'd probably take a couple of pounds of alum and a few yards of wire.'

'Again going on about your tawing and stuffing? Don't tell me you've dragged another one home! We've already got three stiffs on the porch. What for? What do you want with all these corpses? This isn't a forester's lodge. Wiolka is walking around drunk from all that glue.'

My father smirked under his moustache, kissed my mother on the cheek and led her out onto the porch.

He opened the cupboard, and out fell the stiffened claws of eviscerated hares, pheasants, martens, goshawks, buzzards and kestrels.

'Look at this.' He pulled out a dead goshawk, spread out its slightly stiffened dark blue wings and looked at them with admiration. 'I promised to prepare this beauty for the director of the paper mill. If I do a good job, I might get a pay rise. This is the last time, I swear to you. You know I can't live without it. Gypsy blood! My grandfather Szydło, the one who raised me, he was also into stuffing birds, and my great-grandfather would bring skins to trade at the market in Siewierz.'

My mother narrowed her green eyes. The bit about a higher salary clearly persuaded her because she changed her tone.

'Okay, fine, but this ghastly bird is the last. You can stuff the rest in the barn!'

She went back to the kitchen and began to singe a plucked hen over the stove. The fire blazed between the partly open stove lids. The smell of scorched skin and burnt newspapers filled the house.

I heard the rustle of a nylon housecoat. My mother pulled the warm duvet off me and laid it out on chairs arranged together by the side of the bed. Even though it was summer, she didn't air out the bedding on the fence on Sundays because, as she used to say, it would be a disgrace to display all that clobber outside on the Lord's day.

After I washed and put on a puff-sleeved blouse, a checked mid-length skirt and knee-high socks, my grandmother called me into her room. She pulled out her purse from under the straw mattress, gave me a banknote for the collection tray, verified that I had plaited my unruly hair and sent me off to church.

Still feeling a bit sleepy, I walked down the cobbled road, chewing dried pears. Near the fire station, the ice-cream man's painted van sounded its horn. I glanced at the banknote and inwardly prayed that this week I wouldn't yield to temptation to use the collection money to buy three scoops of ice cream – and then have to own up to it at confession.

'Well, well, who do we have here? Rysiek's daughter, I see,' smiled the ice-cream man. 'Do you know how my hare is doing? Is it ready yet?'

I shrugged. 'Dad was reinforcing it a couple of days ago, so I guess it'll be done soon.'

I took my ice cream and turned by the holy spring towards the lane that crossed the road to St Anthony's Basilica.

After Mass, I wanted to slip away to my hiding place in a pile of breeze blocks to read my comics about Tytus, Romek and A'Tomek, but an acquaintance of my grandmother's was cycling beside me, watching me closely. On my way home, I picked two parasol mushrooms which had grown in the ditch, in the exact spot where our neighbour would dump animal slurry. When I got home, I steeped them in milk, put a lid over them and left them in a cool room. Then I sat at the table, which was set with plates full of pasta, laid my head down on the surface and felt the pulsating of the wood. In its cracks and knots, christenings, wakes and name-day celebrations were in full swing, and woodworms were playing dodgeball using poppy seeds that had fallen from the crusts of freshly baked bread.

'Wiolka, watch where you put your head. Your hair will get into the pasta,' my mother admonished me. I woke up. Golden light was gliding along the wall unit, the crystal, the glass fish, the stoneware cups.

After scrubbing the burnt pan with sand in the company of insatiable chickens, ducks and turkeys, my mother filched a few cigarettes from my father's jacket pocket and disappeared. I finished the washing up and went off to look for bantam hens' eggs among the nettles because on Sundays I always felt like *kogel-mogel*, which I would scoop up with a teaspoon and dip in freshly brewed coffee.

When I got back, my father removed the tablecloth, covered the table with newspapers, washed his hands

thoroughly like a surgeon and began making an incision
in the goshawk's belly with his penknife, taking care not
to stain its shiny down with blood. He spent over an
hour removing the entrails, which he threw into a tin
bucket under the table. The bird, stripped of its light
pink flesh, bones and fat, lay on a newspaper. After carefully flipping it inside out, my father rubbed the skin
with alum, which he kept in a pickle jar. The climax of
the process was the preparation of a wire frame to replace
the bird's skeleton. This activity demanded considerable
concentration, so my father usually took a break at this
point, reached for the cigarettes in his jacket and told me
to brew him a cup of strong tea with five teaspoons of
sugar. When preparing animals, he always liked to drink
this sort of sickly sweet syrup.

Smoking, he would narrow his eyes and scrutinise the
dead bird drying on the warm stovepipe. Then he'd get
his toolbox from under the bed and start trimming pieces
of golden wire with his pliers. I liked the metal frame
much more than the bones, which reeked of coagulated
blood. After slipping what remained of the goshawk
over the structure, he would stuff it with wadding, using
tweezers to push cotton wool into places that were harder
to reach. Finally, he sewed up the skin with fine thread
and affixed ruffled feathers with Butapren glue. To finish things off, he inserted suitably painted glass balls into

the eye sockets. Using the thin wires sticking out of the talons, he attached the goshawk to a birch bough that had been marked by a hot poker with his initials: RR.

The clock struck seven. My father told me to salt the table and scrub it thoroughly, while he himself took his paints and moved to the porch to work on the final touch-ups under the 200-watt bulb. Right after I put the tablecloth back on the table, my mother came back with a basket of plums. She called me into the kitchen to help prepare supper. I cut the bread and spread paprikash paste onto the slices. When I returned to the dining room with a plateful of sandwiches, my father was no longer sitting at the table; he was dozing on the sofa. The goshawk, with its artificially spread wings, soared above him.

Waiting for the Popemobile

IN THE SAME YEAR THAT A RUMOUR SPREAD
through Hektary that the Pope would drive past our
village, my father took over the running of the farm
and, to my grandmother's dismay, began to introduce
reforms, gradually turning our homestead into an
unruly and exuberant zoo. It wasn't just beehives and
cages with goldfinches, canaries and rabbits, or a dovecote in the attic, where clumsy nestlings hatched out of
delicate eggs that looked like table-tennis balls. In the
middle of February, right after my birthday, wanting to
cheer me up after the loss of Blacky, Dad pulled out of
his jacket a little soggy, squeaking ball of fluff, which
by the warmth of the stove gradually began to turn
into a several-weeks-old Tatra sheepdog. We called him
Bear.

That spring, my father got hold of an excavator and
widened the pond behind our house, close to the road.

My mother forbade me from going anywhere near it, but after she left for work I would sneak out to what now looked like a trapezium-shaped clay-pit pool. I would crouch by the mound of excavated soil, holding on to the stubs of whitewashed trees or clumps of sweet flag surrounded by frogspawn, and I would watch the wrinkles made on the water by pond skaters.

One Sunday just before the arrival of the Pope, my father handed me the binoculars and told me to watch the nearby field. 'A good opportunity came up, so I got you a number in exchange for a litre of vodka,' he whispered, pointing at the farthest meadow, sprinkled with dandelions. 'That's where we'll build a new house.'

I didn't know what this 'getting a number' involved, but I had come to think that since his return from military detention, Dad had been living in two houses: one was a stone ruin wobbling unsteadily over its limestone foundations, while the other, which for years had been forming in his head, was a clean brick house with central heating, an attic scented with resin and a shiny bathroom tiled from floor to ceiling.

That evening, I noticed that my grandmother had prepared a cake and had washed the floor with diluted vinegar, which usually heralded the imminent arrival of guests. Sure enough, shortly afterwards, women from the village began to arrive: my grandmother's two sisters,

Zofia and Salomea, almost all of our female neighbours from Hektary and, to my surprise, Stasikowa the dressmaker, who seldom dropped in on anyone because she was buried up to her ears in work. Including Mum, there were probably a dozen women at our house. They had all brought cloth pouches and farm sieves, which were covered with kerchiefs.

I thought this might be some sort of feathering evening, even though nobody in Hektary ever got together to tear up feathers in June. Instead of feathers, the women started to toss out of their sieves various scraps of colourful fabrics, fragments of dresses, housecoats, christening shawls, curtains, embroidered wall hangings and fringes left over from Easter Turk costumes, whatever they happened to have at home, and under Stasikowa's direction they set about sewing pennants for bunting to adorn the roadside during Pope John Paul II's visit to Poland.

When the line of bunting was nearly ready, snaking around two rooms, the hallway and the porch, my grandmother started to lay out refreshments on the dresser and the windowsills, while Mum took out a bottle wrapped in a rag from a secret cranny in the kitchen.

'Well, girls, shall we drink to the Holy Father's health?' she proposed. She didn't have to say it twice. The women set aside their thimbles, rags and thread, made themselves comfortable and, sipping the home-made egg liqueur, began to spin their tales.

'Since my old man died, I can't be bothered to melt caramel to wax the hair over my lip,' confessed the dressmaker in her low voice, hemming the last edge of a pennant. 'I don't scrub my heels with ash, I don't rinse my hair with camomile tea, I don't dream at dawn about falling from a ladder. My nose has grown longer, my breasts have sagged – in other words, girls, I'm on the way out.' She laughed hoarsely.

'Oh, come on now, you want to leave us behind? Who else would help us when we need it? Who would do our sewing for weddings and First Communions? You've managed so long without a bloke, surely you can bear being alone in this world a while longer,' said my grandmother.

'And how's little Wiola?' my grandmother's elder sister, Salomea, asked her. 'Has Aunt Flo come to visit her yet? You know, her aunt from America... her blood relation...'

'How would I know?'

The women looked at me searchingly, and I blushed all the way to the tips of my ears, because even though I didn't understand a thing from all this mysterious talk about an aunt from America, I intuitively felt that something important was at stake. I moved Bear off my knees, and as he played with scraps of cloth under the table I pondered what blood relation could possibly come to visit me. Maybe they were talking about my grandfather's paternal uncle's wife, who had stashed tsarist roubles in her stockings and fled to Canada during a dysentery epidemic. But she would have had to be about a hundred and twenty.

'Keep on sewing, girls, keep on sewing, 'cause you're chinwagging and dawdling, and the boys will be here in no time to get the bunting,' said my grandmother's other sister, Zofia, coming to my rescue.

Someone knocked on the door, and there was a commotion on the porch. Three men stuffed the line of bunting into a jute sack and went to hang it up by the side of the road. Later it turned out that the men whose task it was to destroy the decorations had already been waiting for them on the far side of the crossing.

In the morning, I rushed to the road with Bear to welcome the Pope, carrying a paper pennant with the Vatican's coat of arms which I had bought at the corner shop. All that was left of the half-mile of bunting were muddy shreds soaking in the ditch next to empty vodka bottles and cigarette ends. I waited for the Popemobile for several hours. It kept drizzling. Bear started to look the way he did the day Dad brought him home. The asphalt glistened like the skin of an aubergine. A delayed coach plastered with images of the Holy Father drove past from the direction of Katowice carrying pilgrims to the Jasna Góra Monastery in Częstochowa, then the blue-and-white uniforms of the junior cycle club from Poraj flashed before my eyes, then came Gienek the Combine Driver, who usually headed to the Jupiter Inn around that time for lunch, and two tractors and a lorry with the words, 'Buy your clothes at CDT'. When the rain settled in for good, I took shelter with Bear under the lean-to roof of the inn, inhaling the aroma of cabbage rolls and hunter's stew, and the buffet lady told me to go home for lunch because they said on television that the Pope had flown that morning to Częstochowa in a helicopter.

The Little Paint Girl

ONE DAY IN THE MIDDLE OF JULY, MY FATHER GOT
back from work early, and as he replaced the flypaper
around the ceiling lamps, he said to my mother that
martial law in Poland would end in a couple of days. I was
nine, and even though I could remember the day when
the children's show *Telemorning* had failed to appear on
the telly, I still had no idea what he was talking about.
I wondered why my grandfather, who was an expert
when it came to the previous two wars and who knew
all the Resistance songs and all the caves in the Jurassic
Uplands, where he had hidden after his escape from a
camp, never mentioned this martial law. I thought that
he was interested in politics because one day, when no
one was home, he called my grandmother and me into
the kitchen, put two coffee beans on top of a ten-złoty
banknote, so that General Bem was transformed into
General Jaruzelski, with his dark glasses, and burst out

laughing so hard that the clips of his braces nearly popped open.

That night, my father, who belonged to the work security force, did not put on his armband and go to take up his post by the fire station and the co-op. Instead, he spread out his tools on the lino and started weaving a trap out of copper wire for the muskrats, who since the spring had been waging a hit-and-run campaign against him near our pond. When the trap started to look like a golden hourglass, I mustered the courage to ask him who his enemy was, under martial law. He gave me a frightened look and said that if I ever asked that question again, I would get a proper spanking.

On the tenth of August, we walked two and a half miles to the parish fair at St Lawrence's in Cynków. At the market stalls, arranged in two rows near the wooden church, I bought a barometer in the shape of a Tatra mountain cabin, with a highland woman looking out to indicate rain and a man emerging to forecast sunshine, as well as a string of little bagels and a raffle ticket. I slipped the raffle ticket into the pocket of my dress and hid behind the shooting gallery, so as not to have to show it to the other children, just in case I won, say, an enamelled pot or a bobble-head bulldog. As it happened, my number turned out to correspond to a set of Old Holland Classic Colours oil paints. I raced to tell my parents, who were playing cards with some friends near the wooden deer feeder. I showed them my prize. Uncle Lolek gave my father an amused pat on the back and said, 'Well, Rysiek, you have an artist on your hands.'

We walked back through the fields and got home before midnight. Dad lay down on the sofa in his suit and started playing prison ballads on a lime-tree leaf, while Mum and Bear, who had been let off his chain specially for this occasion, formed his faithful audience. I shut myself in the dining room, made a makeshift mosquito net out of a sheer curtain and with reverence laid out seventeen tubes of paint on top of a duvet. Seventeen because one was missing. The English names of the colours made me think of distant planets: 'cyclamen', 'ultramarine', 'umber'. I tried to squeeze out a bit of paint onto a straw mat, but all that leaked out of the tubes were colourless drops of viscous liquid. It turned out that the paints which the priest from St Lawrence's parish had donated to the raffle had come from gift parcels from the West and were past their expiry date.

I went back to school after the summer holidays and forgot about painting – until I spotted an announcement for an art competition on the noticeboard in the common room. The theme was to be 'Moscow through your eyes'; the deadline was the end of October 1983.

Obviously, I had to enter. In January, I had won a province-wide competition titled 'Threats around your farm'. I had painted a potato beetle climbing out of an empty Coca-Cola bottle. Nobody believed that I had really seen my grandfather collecting potato beetles in just such a bottle. The jury at the provincial level concluded that my drawing 'portrayed, in a deeply metaphorical manner, the crusade of the imperialist beetle'. If it hadn't been for the fact that my father had been boasting to his co-workers that he was distantly related to the Sinti Gypsies, my work might have even made it onto postage stamps. In any case, it all ended very well for me. My mother stopped dragging me to evening religion classes in the shack by the forest, and I got a rucksack and a box of chocolates from the competition organisers.

Three weeks after the results of the 'Threats around your farm' contest were published, a letter came to my school. The headmistress announced during assembly that a special sub-committee of the committee for the promotion of culture in the province of Silesia had chosen to send me to an outdoor painting workshop in nearby Lubliniec for the winter break. This was a serious blow. The entire school laughed at me: I was going to spend a week in the loony bin, since Lubliniec was home to a psychiatric ward. On top of that, the holiday centre in which we were lodged was right next door to an army unit, and as we walked around the woods in search of inspiration, soldiers at the training ground were firing blanks, practice bullets were whistling over my head, and I couldn't concentrate. However, the week-long workshop turned out to be a splendid adventure because the common room had satellite TV and a VCR. In my free time, when I wasn't watching films, I painted a series depicting the derelict Lubliniec distillery, but this time I got only a special mention, and instead of my longed-for oil paints, I came home with a certificate and a glossy book about the Russian painter Vasily Surikov, whom I'd never heard of before.

Third time lucky, I thought to myself, and decided to enter the competition entitled 'Moscow through your eyes'. I didn't know what the capital of the socialist republics looked like, and the pictures that accompanied the readings in my Russian textbook were rather blurry. Fortunately, my form teacher, Mrs Walo, who also ran the art club, brought me some colour postcards showing the Kremlin and St Basil's Cathedral. I spread out newspapers on the table and went on painting a panorama of Moscow until two in the morning, when the power was cut.

The next day at school, I left my bag on the floor during the lunch break. Big Witek sat on it, and my spare pen cartridges, which were in the same compartment as my painting for the competition, leaked all their ink. I went pale. The picture was ruined. I went to the toilet and smudged the ink on the page with a tissue. It looked as if the capital of the Union of Soviet Socialist Republics was being engulfed by a viscous ocean of indigo. I left the picture to dry out by the tile stove. During the next break, I put it in a brown envelope and handed it over to Mrs Walo. She didn't even glance inside; she stamped it with the Wojsławice Primary School's emblem and hurried off to the post office.

A month later, a strange man appeared at the school. Nothing about him matched anything else: he had gentle facial features and pointy ears; he was dressed in a black turtleneck and a light-coloured suit jacket; his trousers were neatly creased but his shoes were muddy. He went straight to the headmistress's office.

'Rogalówna!' I heard. I had been summoned.

I ran along gladly because I thought I was going to get some sort of prize again. Through the clouds of cigarette smoke, I saw Mrs Walo's tear-smeared face. My *Moscow* lay on the desk. The headmistress led the jittery teacher out of the room.

After they left, the stranger said, 'I've made a special trip all the way from the provincial government office to reward your work.'

I imagined he would present me with a new set of oil paints and bars of Wedel milk chocolate with hazelnuts, or a bag of sweets. I swallowed – and he really did pull out some chocolate from his briefcase. He slowly unwrapped the silver foil. The velvety scent of cocoa filled the office.

'Go on, help yourself.' He held the desecrated bar right under my nose. I took three squares. My stomach was rumbling. I was hungry because I hadn't eaten breakfast that morning.

'Have you ever been to Moscow, Wiola?'

'No.'

The chocolate melted pleasantly in my mouth.

'And who might have given you this… interesting idea? Was it your parents? Or maybe the teacher who runs the art club? What's her name – Mrs Walo?'

Don't start a sentence with 'and', I thought.

'That's how I imagined Moscow myself, sir.' I decided not to mention the whole business with my school bag, Big Witek and the ink.

'But why so… so catastrophically?'

'So *what*?'

'Why so gloomily?'

Why did the chicken cross the road? I sighed and remembered Mrs Walo's teary face. I didn't trust this man, but I reached for another square of chocolate.

'If you tell me who gave you this idea, the competition organisers will send you on a free trip to Moscow. What do you say to that? You could see the Kremlin!'

He looked at me slyly and smiled, showing his crooked teeth. This conversation was wearing me out. I started shifting from foot to foot. I felt nauseous from the chocolate, and to make things worse, the man kept on muttering something and walking around in circles. As he held the drawing up to my face, someone knocked on the door. A shaggy head peeked into the room.

'Boss, I have some bad news. I swear I just popped to the gents' for a minute, and when I got back, there were two punctured tyres.'

'Don't bother me right now; you know what to do. This always happens. Put the spares on.'

'Yessir, right away.'

The shaggy head disappeared and I felt faint. I heard the questions 'Who?' 'Well, who?' 'When?' 'Why?'

I leaned over the desk and saw my pale reflection in the polished surface. A fly sat on top of the painting, in the darkest nook of the Red Square, and proceeded to crawl freely over the ink-flooded Spasskaya Tower. I felt a cramp in my stomach, and then my brown vomit covered the light part of the city.

The school nurse was called, and I was sat in an armchair and plied with bitter stomach drops diluted in water. I glanced at the Polish coat of arms hanging over the door frame. The crownless eagle was blurring into the red background. When I recovered, the caretaker walked me home. In the yard, I chased away hissing geese with my school bag, stepped up onto the porch and walked through the hallway, which stank of mouse droppings, and into the kitchen. I nodded hello to my mother, threw down my school bag by the dresser, climbed the ladder up to the attic, lay down beside the pigeon cage on sacks filled with wheat and thought that on Sunday I would travel to Olsztyn and find a cave for myself there, just like my grandfather.

In the weeks that followed, the headmistress dissolved the school art club, and I did not participate in any more painting competitions. Once in a while, in secret, Miss Dorota from our neighbourhood would have me decorate a letter to her boyfriend, who was stationed with the army unit in Lubliniec. I also painted a skull for Big Witek on the ceiling of his room, in exchange for three matchbox labels, which I was collecting.

On the tenth of December, Lech Wałęsa received the Nobel Peace Prize and I stayed behind at school for a Christmas play rehearsal. Dad was supposed to pick me up at six o'clock, but the bus which he usually took from the paper mill hadn't come. I was standing by myself at the bus stop, shifting from foot to foot. The water dripping from the tap by the fire station had started to form an icicle in the freezing cold. In the shop across the street, the windows had frosted over. The street lights flickered and flickered, and then went out. The woman from the shop cracked open the door and stuck out her head, bundled up in a fox-fur hat.

'What are you doing here, my child, all alone? Go home, or you'll freeze in this chill!' she shouted.

I was very cold and hungry, so I decided to take her advice – to stop waiting for Dad and walk home by the shortcut through the farm fields. It didn't occur to me, however, that I would have to wade through snowdrifts in the dark. Just before I reached the state-owned farm, I slipped, hit the back of my head on a stone, and then fell into a huge snowdrift and couldn't dig myself out. One of my boots slipped off while I was struggling in the snow. My soaked tights were starting to freeze. My toes went numb. I felt faint.

Suddenly, I was standing in Red Square, dressed in an embroidered vest and a carmine headscarf. My felt boots were muddied. It was an autumn morning, and the Orthodox church shimmered blue and gold in the sun. I didn't know why I had come here with my grandparents, and I stood in the crowd frightened. The stench of horse dung and human sweat mingled with the smell of hot wax. I grabbed my grandmother's hand.

In the distance, someone was swinging from a gallows like a scrap of wet canvas. My grandmother was crying terribly; she had covered her face and was squeezing a candle in one hand, without even noticing the hot wax dripping onto her skin.

When I came to, I realised I was in Hektary, not in Moscow, and I had simply dreamt about one of Vasily Surikov's paintings, the one about the execution of the Streltsy. I was still lying in the snowdrift, but I wasn't cold any more and I didn't feel any pain in my toes. All of a sudden, I noticed the flash of a torch.

'Boss, should I rescue her before she freezes?'

I thought I heard the driver of the man from the provincial government, the one who had questioned me about *Moscow* at school a few weeks earlier. I could smell petrol, vodka and cigarettes. Someone pulled me out of the snowdrift and moved me to the road. That's where my father, on his way back from work, found me a quarter of an hour later. He immediately wrapped me up in his trench coat and carried me home piggyback.

After midnight, Mum ran over to the neighbour who made moonshine in his cellar and brought back two bottles. She poured out half a pint, mixed in strong tea and sugar, and served it to Dad, who still couldn't calm down after finding me lying half-dead in the road. She rubbed the rest of the moonshine into my feet. After the application of all possible remedies – including a poultice of parboiled cabbage leaves on my calves and a greasing with mutton and dog tallow – I regained the feeling in my toes.

A Picture Pays a Visit

WHEN THE PRIEST ANNOUNCED THAT THE PICTURE
of Our Lady from St Anthony's Basilica would pay a
visit to Hektary, my mother and grandmother set about
cleaning our neglected house at once: they started
washing the grimy walls, waxing the floors, sweeping
away spiderwebs from the ceilings and rubbish from
under the beds, polishing the windowpanes with de-
natured alcohol and newspapers, changing the musty
straw in the mattresses and spraying all the rooms with
fly killer.

'We can't have bugs nesting in the corners when
the Most Holy of Virgins crosses our threshold,' my
grandmother kept saying. She wiped plant leaves with
cheesecloth and used a blessed palm frond to sprinkle
the porch and the thresholds, so that flies wouldn't come
into our house. But the flies didn't give two hoots about
my grandmother's prestidigitation: they kept flying in as

usual through the holes in the net curtain and circling around the ceiling lamp.

My grandmother reached into the wardrobe for the crucifix and the holy-water sprinkler, which had been wrapped in a shawl, then put a small table in the dining room, laid out a tablecloth and covered it with periwinkles and freesias, which my mother had brought back specially for this occasion from the greenhouse in the neighbouring village. I was squeezed into my cousin's First Communion dress and told to stand nice and straight beside the wall unit, which was polished to a shine.

In the meantime, the holy image, encased in a chest and placed in a litter, was making the rounds through Hektary. A strange procession plodded behind it, of the same sort as for the blessing of the fields. The curate's white robe flickered between the trees. The firemen's helmets glinted in the sun, casting bright reflections. At the last minute, some people tried to sweep their yards, air out their houses, drive poultry back into pens. Children kept getting lost and found. Untethered, thirsty cows mooed in the pastures. Dogs broke from their chains and ran around the village, astounded by their unexpected freedom.

In the late afternoon, my grandfather burst into the house in muddy shoes and bellowed, 'For Chrissake, women, tie up that cow right quick because she's parked herself by the gate, blocking the way in.'

'Holy Mother of God, they're coming! They're coming! I can already see them on the hill!' cried my grandmother.

My father, an inveterate atheist, grabbed a piece of poppyseed cake from the kitchen and fled to the barn. A moment later, our yard was filled with singing: 'O Madonna, O Black Madonna, how good it is to be Your child.' The curate entered first, stumbling over the threshold, and the crowd following him poured onto the porch and into the hallway, the kitchen, the dining room and the bedroom. The firemen carried in the chest, covered with tulle, and set it down on the waiting altar. My mother lit candles and turned on the light, which surprised me because she rarely used it during the day. An hour later, the curate blessed the assembled company and then returned to the presbytery with the sacristan in a Fiat, but the rattling off of prayers continued at our house until dusk. Timidly, my mother began to read the Litany of the Blessed Virgin from the service book: 'Mother undefiled, Mother most amiable, Mother most admirable, Mother of good counsel, house of gold, Ark of the Covenant, gate of Heaven, morning star...'

After the priest had left, everyone relaxed. People started to reach for the cake and sit down on the lino and the windowsills. Children ran outside to play on the sand heap by the fence. Someone let the chickens out of the pigsty. I leaned against the wall, chewing on the edge of a tablecloth. Even though I was seriously frightened, I desperately wanted to peek inside the tulle-covered box. I thought it might contain some sort of little green alien, smelling of wax, mothballs and dust. When I leaned forward, the lights went out.

'The fuses are buggered.'

'Is it an overload?'

'Maybe it's the Łagisza power station?'

'Do you have matches?'

'Light a candle.'

The whispers came from the kitchen, the hallway, the porch – until finally the spell of peregrination was broken. The candles, which had melted down during the long hours of prayer, sputtered and spluttered and then also went out. My stomach growled. In the semi-darkness, individual figures slunk off into the yard.

'Janek, go and see what's up with that fuse box!' shouted my aunt to her husband the electrician. I heard a clatter behind the curtain in the hallway, the metallic sound of a knocked-over bucket of urine, swearing and laughter.

'All our daily deeds...' my mother intoned in an attempt to save the situation, but only a few people took up the tune.

It occurred to me that the sudden power cut was my father's doing: impatient for supper, he must have come into the hallway through the little door by the pigsty and unscrewed the fuses. I smiled to myself. After a quarter of an hour, before the dazzling lights came back on, the weary visitors began to disperse and go home. My mother knelt before the holy picture, crossed herself and then chased us out of the dining room, put a sheer curtain over the Most Holy of Virgins, so that flies wouldn't sit on her, turned off the lights and went to the kitchen to prepare supper.

Whitsunday

IN MAY 1984, I SET OUT FOR CHURCH CARRYING A
bundle of sweet flag, which I had picked that morning
by the pond and adorned with ribbons. Water dripped
from the bouquet onto my Sunday shoes. The church
was filled with the smell of sweet flag leaves and silt, like
a drying bog. My head started to spin. When the parish
priest began to read a passage about the Descent of the
Holy Spirit, the boat-shaped pulpit sailed off with him
into the unknown. I slid from the bench down to the
floor. They carried me outside. A woman drew a cross
on my forehead with her spit.

'We must tie a red ribbon in her hair and break the
spell,' she said, turning to the gawkers.

A few days later, my mother made an appointment
for a private consultation with Dr Kwiecień. The sixty-
year-old physician had the kindly face of Willy from *Maya
the Bee*, but I saw through him right away, glowering at

his clean-shaven, purplish cheeks. This weasel told my mother to wait in the hallway, where a large rubber plant stood next to a shelf, and led me to the consulting room, behind a privacy screen. He wiped the earpieces of his stethoscope on his white coat and came up so close to me that I could smell his perfume. He undid his fly, moved even closer and put his penis in my hand, like a roll of modelling clay. I jumped back and kicked his leg as hard as I could. The squeal of a slaughtered piglet must have been heard throughout the entire building. Alarmed, my mother came into the room. Kwiecień did up his fly and peeped out from behind the screen. A moment later, he sat down at his desk and started grumbling that I was a spoiled brat, since I had kicked his shin for no reason when he tried to examine my lymph nodes. He showed the red mark to my mother. Then suddenly he turned mild as an angel and declared that I seemed healthy but that I might be anaemic, which would explain my excessive irritability and fainting spells. He handed my mother a blood-test form.

'After you pick up the results, please come back to see me with your daughter.'

We were walking home. The afternoon sun was shining through the branches of the birch trees growing by the road, rubber-stamping the cream-coloured boughs with purple marks. My mother was silent for a long time.

When we reached Boży Stok, she broke off a withy and shoved it right under my nose.

'You see this? If you kick anyone again, I'll give you a proper whipping, understood?'

The following day, I came down with a high fever. I stayed home alone and lay in bed, sipping lime-flower tea. Around noon, I put an immersion heater in a metal mug, boiled some water and dipped a thermometer into the liquid. The mercury container burst. Silver beads spilled onto the bedding. I gathered them up. I hesitated for an instant, but when I remembered Kwiecień's face, I swallowed the balls like caplets and fell asleep. I woke up a few hours later with my head swimming. I vomited as if I were trying to spit out my insides. In the end, I confessed to my parents, who had just come home from work, that I had swallowed mercury. My father dashed off to the village mayor's house to call an ambulance.

The room at the children's ward of the Lubliniec county hospital resembled a lime kiln in the Jurassic Uplands. Glaring light glided along the walls, condensed in the catheter of the IV drip and poured into the barely visible vein in my left wrist through plastic tubes. My mother's face, red from crying, seemed ten years older in the fluorescent glow.

After a while, a skinny doctor arrived and took my mother aside. As he spoke, his Adam's apple bobbed up and down, as if he had swallowed a frog. Pretending to be asleep, I eavesdropped on their conversation: 'Elemental mercury is not dangerous... The intestines cannot absorb it... We'll keep checking... We'll keep checking every few hours.'

After the doctor left, my mother looked at me with reproach. I wanted to explain everything, but I didn't get a chance. In the neighbouring bed, a girl with crimson blisters around her mouth, who had swallowed some caustic potato-beetle poison, started to choke. There was a commotion. They took her away to a different ward.

The visiting hours ended at seven. Mum left a jar of homemade redcurrant juice on the bedside table and went home. A nurse disconnected the drip and turned off the light. I was alone at last. The bare walls flashed and shifted in front of my eyes like an origami fortune teller. The last of the light seeped out onto the street, wrapping poplars with copper thread and coming to a halt at the barred windows of the women's prison across from the hospital. I pressed my hot cheek against the cool pane. The prisoners were performing a secret pantomime in their windows. The longest day of my life ended with the Scorpions' ballad 'When the Smoke is Going Down'. Klaus Meine's voice drifted towards me from the nurse's station until, around midnight, all went quiet.

An Easter Pasha

IT WAS THE MIDDLE OF FEBRUARY AND SLEET WAS falling, even though since the morning my Tatra cabin barometer had had the highland man looking out to forecast sunshine. My grandmother added cream to the sour rye and potato soup and opened the window a crack. The sooty net curtains billowed out like fish swim bladders. My grandfather came home soaking wet, hung his hat on the back of a chair and proceeded to scoop mushroom pieces out of the soup with a ladle.

'Get outta here!' my grandmother scolded him.

My grandfather put on the face of a naughty child caught in the act, grabbed the fly swatter and chased away a cloud of flies that had been feeding on sugar crystals spilled on the plastic tablecloth.

'What's got into you, Władek?' my grandmother asked.

'The Director told me to play.'

'To play what?'

'To play in a play.'

He threw the swatter down on the windowsill, spat in the half-open ash pan, put his hat back on and went out again.

The next day, the buffet lady from the Jupiter Inn reported to my grandmother that the Director had bought my grandfather two doubles of vodka and spent a long time trying to persuade him to take part in some sort of performance at the Farmers' Club. But even the buffet lady didn't know exactly how this Director had found himself in Hektary and what sorts of things he directed or steered – apart from his Fiat 125p – though people said that he was a 'delegate' who'd been sent from somewhere. In practice, he organised social events and raffles, he had procured a VHS player for the community hall at the fire station, and the previous year he had invited Mum on a culinary course at the Countrywomen's Association, where he demonstrated, among other things, how to make lemon soup. As a matter of fact, the words 'lemon soup' were later forbidden in our house – after a Christmas party during which Mum was stuck dancing a charity waltz with the Director.

My grandfather clearly wasn't thrilled at the prospect of taking part in the show, but he was trying not to let on. Admittedly, he did like to perform, and he was known in the village for his appearances at harvest festivals and weddings and at the inn, where he'd pop in once a month after getting his pension and sing old Resistance songs and folk ballads until dawn. The problem was that my grandfather couldn't stand the Director, who had to stick his nose into every celebration in Hektary. Shortly before, for example, he had turned up at a firemen's meeting, as if by accident, and declared that the Easter Turks were a nonsense tradition which had to be abolished, since it wasn't Turkish but Roman guards who had kept watch over the tomb of Jesus in Jerusalem. My grandfather was furious because he had always known, ever since he was a child, that the Easter Turks commemorated the victory of the Polish forces at the Battle of Vienna, and the fighting men who returned home a year later, just before Easter, dressed up in the trophy costumes of the Ottoman army.

On Good Friday, for as long as I could remember, my grandfather would put on a patterned tunic and a fringed waistcoat. Armed with a colourful Easter 'palm' – which was in fact a huge sceptre made from branches, flowers and leaves – he would go with the other firemen to guard the Holy Sepulchre at St Anthony's Basilica. The following night, when the parish priest announced the good news during the Easter Vigil, the Turks would remove the black mourning ribbon from their flag and would all drop down to the floor with such a thud that pieces of amber would tumble from the necklaces adorning St Anthony of Padua's altar, and votive offerings pinned to red velvet would curl up like aspen leaves. After the service, the Turks would form two rows, one on each side of the path in front of the church, and with their Easter palms they would gently poke at the shoes of selected girls, as if to confer on them a special blessing for the coming spring.

I was certain that my grandfather, rifleman of the 74th Regiment of the Lubliniec Infantry, former Stalag prisoner, tile-stove builder, carpenter, singer and Easter pasha all rolled into one, who up to now had never let anyone get the better of him, would sooner or later pull a fast one on the Director. Yet nothing happened. My grandfather obediently attended the rehearsals at the fire station, did everything the Director asked and practised his song in the mow of the barn:

> *There were red roses and poppies and lilacs,*
> *smelling beautifully in a soldier's song,*
> *but in none of the melodies could flower*
> *any yellow marsh marigolds.*

In the afternoon on the eighth of March, the sun came out, even though since the morning my Tatra cabin barometer had had the highland woman looking out to forecast rain. Smudged posters stuck to posts were advertising a musical production at the Farmers' Club called *Yellow Marsh Marigolds*, directed by none other than the Director. As usual on International Women's Day, Mum was staying late at work to celebrate the occasion, my father had slunk off to go fishing, and only my grandmother and I remained at our posts at home to feed the chickens, milk the cow and help my grandfather with the final preparations for the performance.

After lunch, my grandfather gave my grandmother a shawl with a red poppy motif and golden thread, so she sang to herself merrily as she ironed his shirt, which she then carefully laid out on the bedspread. His polished shoes were drying by the stove, next to the cat. Around five, she suddenly looked at my grandfather and bellowed so loud that flies almost dropped from the flypaper and the ceiling almost lost the rest of its whitewash: 'Jesus Christ, Władek! You gotta go in an hour and you still haven't shaved?!'

'No need to yell. I was just about to start.'

He sharpened his razor on a leather belt hung from the door handle, took a shaving brush out of a cocoa tin, picked up the soap, poured warm water from the kettle into a mug and proceeded to shave slowly, checking his reflection in a bicycle mirror. After he put on his suit, fastened his braces and tied his tie, he muttered under his breath, 'Fuck a duck… yellow marsh marigolds and red tomatoes…'

'What tomatoes?' I asked, surprised, but he didn't reply. He put on his polished shoes and with some foam still on his cheek dashed out to the privy behind the barn.

Fifteen minutes passed. Fifteen more minutes passed. I watched the hands of the clock anxiously, since he was gone for quite a long time.

'He'll be back. He's just got caught short from the nerves,' my grandmother kept reassuring me.

At half past six, Bear started to bark. The bantam hens hid under the tarpaulin which covered the remainder of the coal dust left over from the winter. A Fiat 125p pulled up to our gate. Three men got out, dressed to the nines: the Director, the village mayor, carrying a trombone, and the chief of the Volunteer Fire Service, in full dress uniform. My grandmother threw her fur waistcoat over her shoulders and stepped outside.

'Hello, Stefa. Where's Władek?' the village mayor asked.

'Lord be praised. It's been a good half hour since he's gone to the privy and that's the last we've seen of him.'

'Show us the way,' the Director said in a commanding tone. 'And you,' he turned to the chief, 'wait by the gate and keep an eye on the road.'

I ran outside through the little door by the pigsty to watch the whole scene from behind a gooseberry bush, where I'd have a good view.

'Comrade Lubas, you're to report immediately to the Farmers' Club,' the Director hissed and kicked the door to the privy.

'Władek, say something,' I heard my grandmother's voice.

'Open up, Władek, stop fooling around,' the village mayor added.

'Władek, open up, you hear me?' my grandmother tried again.

'Comrade Władysław, we don't have time for this.'

'Lubas, come on, I'll buy you a round,' the chief croaked in his drunkard's voice.

'You've got to talk some sense into him,' the Director said, turning to my grandmother. 'There's no time...'

'Sir!' the chief interrupted him. 'I can see the dignitaries' cars on the hill!'

'What a prick... I knew he'd take me for a ride.'

The Director spat on the daisies that for some reason had bloomed right next to the privy, wiped his muddy loafers with a handful of grass, adjusted the handkerchief in his breast pocket and looked at his watch.

'I've got to get back to the fire station. Keep trying

to persuade him!' he yelled at the village mayor and headed for the gate.

Once the Fiat had disappeared beyond the bridge, the village mayor, who knew my grandfather well and had already suspected something earlier but didn't want to say anything in front of the Director, took a swig out of his hip flask, passed his trombone to my grandmother, grabbed a stick, wedged it into the gap between the door and the wall of the privy and lifted the wooden latch. The door opened slightly. Apart from flies flailing about in spiderwebs, there wasn't a soul inside. On top of a dried-up Easter palm hung my grandfather's hat.

Spiders from Jerusalem

DURING STORMS, I USED TO HIDE IN THE HALLWAY
and play at being Jonah. The shutters up in the attic
would open with a bang. The faded curtain would
billow out like the belly of a whale. The spirit level was
one of its crossed eyes, and the chisels, saws and planes
which hung on the unplastered walls were its fins. Water
dripped from the ceiling and ran down the stone wall.
I could sail to wherever I wanted, in a boat made from
lime-tree wood shavings, but I preferred to stay put on
a sack of oats under the ladder, somewhere between the
rocking horse that had lost its rockers, the rickety cheese
press and the duck sitting on its eggs in an old wooden
washtub. Chaff fell like glitter onto spiderwebs. Above
me, the electricity meter, with its porcelain fuses, ticked
rhythmically. An old slug iron lay on the floor, showing
its teeth. Just as I believed in *bebok*, the Jurassic Uplands
monster which, according to grown-ups, would come

after dark to kidnap naughty children, so I also believed that this iron, true to its name, contained some sort of supernatural slug.

My mother was terrified of storms. As soon as it began to thunder, she'd cross herself, take down the laundry from the lines strung between our two apple trees, bolt shut all the doors and windows, pull plugs out of sockets, hide metal objects and cover the top of the washing machine with a blanket, so that it wouldn't draw lightning. Finally, she would sit on the bed, cover herself with a feather duvet and call me over.

'Be straight with me, have you killed a spider again? You know well enough that it brings thunderstorms.'

'This time it really wasn't me, Mum. I swear, it was Mr Kuzior.'

'Mr Kuzior?' she asked, intrigued.

'In biology class, we were putting cross spiders to sleep with ether, and I think mine breathed in too much, because it never made it out of its matchbox again.'

'Spiders are sacred creatures and it's forbidden to kill them. They saved Our Lady. When the Holy Family was fleeing from Jerusalem, spiders wove such a thick web around the road that the swords of Herod's soldiers couldn't pierce it.'

She would tell me story after story, about how Jesus brought twelve clay birds to life when he was a child, how he hung a pitcher of water on a sunbeam and how he walked on water, how he revived a dried fish and calmed a storm. Eventually she would fall asleep under her duvet, clutching a blessed medallion in her left hand.

Once during a storm, Natka Roszenko came to visit us. We didn't know her well; we just knew that she was one of Cynga's tarts. Cynga had come to the village in the mid-1980s, from who knew where. He had opened the Baboon nightclub in the basement of the forest amphitheatre by the road, and he spent a lot of time at the inn, with the Director and the village mayor. Knowing all this, Mum would still invite Natka over to our house, because the girl sold Hungarian tops and golden-thread shawls at a good price. Besides, how could you not let a person into your home during a storm?

As I sat under the table, playing house, different smells mingled in the stuffy August air: rotting mattress straw, laundry starch, mildew and cat piss. I stuck out my head. The flypaper swayed hypnotically under the ceiling lamp. On the wall, next to the memento of my First Holy Communion, hung a portrait of my grandmother Sabina Szydło. A beautiful, olive-skinned woman in a blue-grey georgette dress with a white lace collar was peeking at me from the picture. Her raven-black plait undulated behind the glass. I missed her, even though I had never met her.

When Mum fell asleep, Natka finished her coffee, crawled under the table and sat down next to me, smiling peculiarly.

'Hey, you, I'll tell you a story. No? Maybe we can play tickles?'

When I didn't reply, Natka brushed aside her dark hair and put a slim arm around me. She smelled of musky perfume. She unbuttoned her blouse and bared her breasts. I shuddered with disgust, but she seemed to interpret this differently. She slipped a hand inside her knickers and half-closed her eyes. Luckily, the storm ended. Someone knocked on the door. My mother turned on the light.

I fled from under the table, shouting, 'Mum, Mum, there are spiders from Jerusalem under there!'

Waves

I HAD BEEN FEELING NAUSEOUS SINCE THE EARLY
morning and I didn't fancy the buckwheat blood pudding
which my grandmother had fried up with onions for
breakfast. I slipped outside and decided to accompany
my grandfather on his expedition to the farm field.
When it turned out that the spring thaws had flooded
the meadows overnight, we turned back. We passed
rotting storage clamps, barberry bushes, a row of apple
trees. Shells of Roman snails crunched under our boots.
The earth smelled of decaying roots, mud, cardamom.

'The Easter of 1913 was also wet,' began my grandfather, who was more talkative than usual that morning.
'The rain kept pouring with only short breaks. Streams
joined up into one fast torrent. There was a flood, and
our neighbours whose house was on low ground – you
know, Balwierka and her family – ran away during the
night and forgot to close their door and windows,

and the water carried off their blessed Easter *babkas* and sausages.'

My grandfather stirred some thick liquid foaming in a ditch with his walking stick. Wire snares danced in the wind like the nooses of invisible hanged men.

'The second wave came right at harvest time. Next to us was the district mayor's field of oats, already in stooks. I tell you, what a sight it was when the water started carrying them off, stook by stook, and they floated towards the river like an army. Some of them got caught on the crowns of trees, broke apart into sheaves and drifted far off, to who knows where.'

'Were you flooded too, in Brudzowice?'

'No, we lived on a hill, but I still kept checking the water level by poking a stick into the ground. In the afternoon, I went to see if the water was rising or falling. I look and there's at least a dozen hares running away from the water. They were hiding in the grass, and I wanted to grab one, but my mother said, "Leave it, they want to live too. Hurry, get the horse and ride out to the cattle in the pasture." Because the cattle were there all summer, and in wet years the foot-and-mouth disease was everywhere.'

I stopped listening to my grandfather when he began recollecting the coming of the third wave. My belly started to hurt. The county helicopter was circling above the fields.

When we got home, the sun was shining over the nearby village of Kolonia. It was nearly noon. Drowsy flies were circling above a steaming pile of dung. Water from the roof was running down drainpipes in streams, battering the young jonquil buds. Snow-white doves strolled about the yard, which looked like a dirty wet rag. Bright patches of inundated fields showed through the gaps in the fence, where boards were missing after my grandfather had chopped them up in February, when the coal had run out. Next to the fence, a small stove with a cracked pipe and flaking patches of patina was dying a slow death. The bones of a rusty harrow protruded from under a tarpaulin among young nettles.

My grandmother scraped the remains of the previous day's potatoes out of a pot to feed the chickens and told me to check if there were any fresh eggs in the pigsty, in the mow or among the nettles. I brought back a few in a farm sieve, sat down on a damp tree stump by the barn and started drawing a spiral on the ground with a stick. Suddenly, I felt a strong cramp in my lower belly. A wave of warmth flooded my crotch and thighs. I ran home.

'Is it possible to bleed to death?' I asked my grandmother. Worried, she stuck her head out of the cellar, where she was picking through potatoes, and when she saw the red stain on my tights, she guessed instantly what was going on. She climbed up the ladder, shuffled off in her wellies to her room and pulled out some starched linen rags from under her straw mattress.

'Wash your tights in cold water, and here, take one of these to put down there. It'll pass in a few days. Your mother can buy you some cotton wool at the corner shop tomorrow, but don't bug me now because the potatoes are going to rot.'

I ran out into the yard. The sun, white and spotted like a goose egg, burned my cheeks. Blowflies were circling above a trough filled with fermented oats. I crawled inside the rabbit cage and fell asleep on the fresh hay. I dreamt about crimson dandelion clocks.

Gienek the Combine Driver

IN FEBRUARY, IT GOT DARK JUST AFTER FOUR.
The air smelled of metal. An almost inaudible blues
hummed in the web of telegraph wires taut from the
frost. The house was filled with the aroma of hot lard.
The cats were pulling out eggshells and empty vanilla-
sugar packets from the coal scuttle and playing with
them under the table. I sat on a stool by the hot stove,
trying to make a brooch for my home economics class
– a butterfly built out of wire, a safety pin and a scrap
of nylon. In a drawer, I had found a few pairs of tights
labelled 'women's, stylish, ladder resistant', which Mum
always got at work for International Women's Day. But
they were all flesh-toned or coffee-brown, and instead
of a butterfly I kept ending up with a moth, which was
'a bit the worse for wear', as my father would describe
himself every Monday, when he came home at dawn
after a little game of poker, red-eyed and yawning, and

made himself some water with baking soda and vinegar for his hangover. Finally, I couldn't take it any more and told Mum, who was cutting strips of rolled-out pastry dough for *faworki*, that I had to drop by the dressmaker's to get a piece of coloured nylon for the brooch.

'You were supposed to help me twist *faworki*, not run around the village,' she said reproachfully.

'But Mum, I have to finish the brooch for school, or I'll fail.'

'Fine, fine, go if you have to, but drink this first.' She handed me a glass of carrot juice, which, as the chief anaemic in the family, I had to drink several times a week, alternating with a flaxseed infusion. Mum would first grate some carrots on a dull grater, then squeeze the orange mush though cheesecloth into a bowl. The juice tasted like rust and soap. I felt queasy at the mere sight of it, but I had to drink it to avoid another visit to Dr Kwiecień.

'Be careful and take the little torch because it's awfully dark out.' She accompanied me all the way to the gate.

I tried skating on the ice-covered path, humming the ballad 'Hey, Gypsy Man, Where Are You Going?' The lights in all the houses in Hektary, Kolonia and Świnica were on. The stench of burnt fat wafted out through chimneys, smoke holes and cracks in windows. People were making sweet treats for Fat Thursday.

All of a sudden, Gienek the Combine Driver emerged out of the darkness. He was walking his bicycle, or rather the bicycle was walking the full two hundred and ninety pounds of Gienek to the Jupiter Inn for beef roulade with cabbage. In the winter, Gienek seemed somehow different from how he was at harvest time, when he'd drive the Farmers' Club combine up to the open door of our barn, all tanned and smiling. Now he looked like a plaster cast of himself: his face was swollen and he was breathing with difficulty. He kept stopping to pull up his heavy-duty work trousers, which were tied with a cord under his belly.

'Hi, Gienek.'

'Who's that? Oh, it's you, sweetie. You're off to religion class?'

'No, religion's on Friday, in the house by the forest. I'm going to Stasikowa's. What's in there?' I pointed at his bag, hoping he'd offer me some orangeade.

'I bought this at the corner shop to warm me up. Want a sip?' He pulled out a green bottle of birch-water aftershave.

'No, thanks. Do you have any sweets?'

'Ha, a little sweet for a little sweetie.' He chuckled, showing the gap in his teeth. Then he fished around in his trouser pocket, pulled out a milk toffee coated with tobacco and chaff and started waving it in front of me.

'How about a little kiss for Gienek?' he teased. 'Come on, don't be like that... give us a kiss!'

'Kiss schmiss!'

I gave him a quick peck on his prickly cheek, grabbed my toffee and dashed off to the dressmaker's – but she wasn't home. The windows were dark. A complex maze of chicken tracks stretched across the ash-strewn path to the barn. There was a note on the door: 'Gone to my sister's to fry doughnuts. Back soon.'

I knew that for Stasikowa the word 'soon' meant a good two hours, so I decided not to wait and turned around to go home. On the way back, I started playing with the torch, illuminating knots in wooden fences and shining it on meadows covered by grey blankets of snow, on which dogs had spread out pig bones left over from the carnival slaughter. I kept turning the light on and off as if I were talking to the leafless trees in Morse code. I stopped by a little bridge to bounce reflections off the freezing stream and noticed some sort of strange bundle lying in the ditch. I would have kept going, but the bundle started to groan. I went down carefully, hanging on to withies sticking out of the snow. It was Gienek. He lay all curled up, clutching the frame of his Ukraina bicycle, as if he were afraid that if he let go he'd tumble into an abyss.

'Gienek, Gienek, wake up,' I said, nudging him

gently. He opened his eyes and belched right in my face, with the sour smell of the inn storeroom on his breath. 'What happened?'

'I slipped as I was coming back from the Jupiter.'

'Just keep lying still. I'll run to get help.'

'Zo... sia, is that you? I'm not ly... ing, I'm float... ing,' he began in a slurred whisper, as if he were trying to swallow something. A drop of bright red blood ran out of his nose.

'Gienek, it's me, Wiolka, Zosia's daughter.'

'Zo... sia... I... I... love ya,' he mumbled and lost consciousness.

I tried to wake him up by shining the torch in his face, but he didn't react. He let go of the leather bag attached to the frame of his bicycle and began floating, floating off to only he knew where.

Pierced Lids

THE LITANY OF THE BLESSED VIRGIN MARY WAS
still ringing in my ears – since, as usual at that time of
the year, I had to listen to it over and over at various
May devotions and do my share of standing in front of
decorated crosses and shrines – when I remembered that
over lunch my father had mentioned a May bug hunt.
I burst into the house like a ball of lightning, grabbed
a screw-top jar off the table and ran to see my father,
who was crouching by a tree stump making a funnel-like
contraption out of wire.

'Can you pierce this?' I put the jar lid on top of the
stump.

'You're going on a May bug hunt?'

'You said it would be a good idea.'

'Yeah, it's high time we got rid of those bloody
things.'

I finished eating a heel of bread, which always tasted

better to me in the dark, and he stopped punching holes in the lid with a nail.

'Enough?' he asked, showing me the lid, riddled with holes like a sieve.

'That's enough, Dad, thanks!'

I screwed the lid onto the jar and strode off to the meadow behind the barn. I got into position on a well-trodden patch of grass, as if in a boxing ring. The May air smelled of jasmine and caramel. Heavy, juice-laden May bugs came flying from the direction of the apple trees. One of them flew right past my temple like a miniature bomber, brushing my face with its wings. I ran around chasing it in the dark, barefoot on the damp grass, until at last – smack, smack – I got it with an open palm. Stunned, it fell down. I picked it up with my bare hands with disgust and threw it into the jar. I continued my hunt for another half an hour, and then I sensed that a change had taken place inside me: I could see everything more clearly and I was more alert as I set my feet down in the dark.

When the jar was swarming with May bugs, I sat down tired next to Bear's kennel. He was rolling around on the ground trying to shake off fleas. The beetles crammed inside the jar looked like reddish balls from a pilled jumper or a puppet made of burrs.

I popped my head into the pigsty. In their

wooden-slatted pen, young turkeys were crowding on the hay, pecking at shredded yarrow. I hesitated. It seemed to me a pity to let the May bugs be devoured. In the end, I unscrewed the jar, dumped the half-dead beetles into the pen and ran off so as not to have to watch the ensuing carnage. On the way to the door, one leg of my trousers got caught on a nail in the chicken ladder. Smack, smack fell the wooden construction, right on top of me.

The dirt floor was warm and damp. The space inside the pigsty glowed brightly, then crumbled into little pieces, like a mosaic. Swallows greeted me with a piercing 'tweet-tweet' from their nest up in the rafters. I felt a tingling around my shoulder blades. Suddenly, I became as light as a scrap of foil. I rose up and sat on the pane of the little window which had been left slightly ajar. I flew out into the yard and circled over the orchard for a while. The sky, like the lid of my jar, was pierced with stars. Through them, a different kind of lining was showing. From up high, I could see the whole village, with the brownish-green forest to the north and the white circles of the dolomite quarry to the east. I had almost broken through the lid, into the second sky, when suddenly – smack, smack – someone smacked me on my feverish cheeks.

I never found out who had dragged me from under the broken ladder and helped me out of the pigsty. The next thing I remember, I was in front of our door. My mother later said that I had come back by myself, dreadfully filthy and with my hair all dishevelled. After a bath, I lay down on the sofa in the dining room, but I couldn't fall asleep for a long time. Something was buzzing in my ears, my head hurt and the skin on my back was burning. A full moon rose over Hektary. On its pale face and on my own, chickenpox spots multiplied.

The Dressmaker's Secret

ONE EVENING, I COULD HARDLY WAIT TO GO TO the dressmaker's, but Mum told me to first put the homemade juice in the cool hallway and then lock the front door from the inside with the bolt. With the bolt because we never used a key, since it was always getting lost somewhere. Mum waited in the yard while I stayed inside and slid the knob along the door. The smell of rust stuck to my fingers. I went behind the hallway curtain, heavy with dirt and fly droppings, and popped through the little door into the pigsty. The chickens were dozing on their ladder. The cow was licking the stone wall. I climbed up to the spiderweb-covered window and jumped out into the icy air.

Mum gave me her hand. We decided to take the shortcut through the fields. Dusk was falling slowly. The frosty grass crunched under our boots. After a fifteen-minute march, the dressmaker's house loomed up in the distance. I knocked a few times. Nobody answered, even though we could hear footsteps in the hallway. A cat jumped out of the dovecote, carrying a nestling in its mouth.

Mum went up to the kitchen window, knocked a few times and whispered, 'Hello? Please open up, it's us. The collection for church repairs isn't until next week, and they won't come checking the meters till tomorrow morning. I know because Janek let it slip.'

A moment later, the door opened. We walked through the hallway, which smelled of sour rye soup, into a bright room. Women's suits, georgette dresses and coats edged with outdated trims and fringes dangled from a broom handle suspended under the ceiling; shrunken ladies' jackets swung like hanged men. A Singer machine stood by the window. There was a little box of pins among the crystal on a dresser shelf, a button jar next to a rucksack on the floor and a mannequin with a cracked head in the corner of the room, draped with ribbons and starched napkins and impaled on a wooden pole like a straw Marzanna effigy drowned each year to celebrate the end of winter. Thimbles, buttons, pins, hook-and-eye clasps, press studs, appliqués, pieces of Velcro and bits of interfacing were sticking out of a cardboard box behind the lamp.

My mother laid a bundle of fabric on the table and

started untying the twine. A pink stream spilled out onto the dirty surface. The dressmaker examined the material with admiration, caressing it as if it were her departed husband's flesh.

'Stunning… And what an even hem! You didn't buy this in Koziegłowy, did you?'

'No, my sister brought it from Katowice. Apparently she queued all day to buy it. So, what do you think? Will it do?' Mum asked with a note of anxiety in her voice. 'Can you make a gown for the end-of-school ball out of it?'

The dressmaker sized me up with her eyes, spread out the fabric, measured it with her forearm and said after a pause, 'Only down to the knees, and that's if I do my best.'

'To the knees? No, that won't… What would the headmistress say? For a ball, it has to be longer. But maybe…' My mother touched her handbag. 'Maybe you could manage to add some other fabric?'

'God forbid! What other fabric? You can tell at a glance that you splashed out at a Pewex shop.'

After that day, I went to the dressmaker's regularly to have fittings. I got used to the smell of her hallway and her house. She would baste the fabric, wrap me in it like a mummy, sew a little. She did everything with great concentration. She'd add things up in her head, draw the pattern on brown paper and then, at the end, she'd sweep all the scraps of fabric from the table to the floor, make some tea, offer me cake, show off her wedding portrait, which hung over the dresser, and reminisce about her husband, Stasik. Then she'd lay out the cards and tell me my fortune, repeating the same thing every time: that I would have two children, a boy and a girl, and that foreign voyages, fame and money awaited me, and when she'd add at the end that I would not find happiness in love, I'd come up with a pretext to leave the table. She would start watching *Return to Eden*, and I'd play with the cat, rummage through bags of fabric scraps, explore all the nooks and crannies pleated by light and shadows. There was only one room I was forbidden to enter. Of course, I tried to disobey several times, but unfortunately the room was always locked.

At night, I often thought about Stasikowa's room. Sometimes I imagined it as a little chapel, except instead of a picture of a saint I would envision a golden cage with parakeets. Other times, I suspected it looked like a theatre dressing room, with costumes and a dressing table. In my dreams, I would enter this room and try on wigs and colourful outfits.

Then one week, I mixed up my days because there was a difficult maths test at school, and I went to see the dressmaker on a Tuesday instead of a Wednesday. To my surprise, the front door was ajar. I went inside. The cat was sleeping on a cushion. The clock was ticking on top of the dresser. In the dressmaker's absence, I decided to peek into the forbidden room. I paused in front of the heavy door, thinking, 'Open, Sesame,' then pushed it and looked inside. The room was in semi-darkness. When my eyes got used to the dim light, I saw what looked like a hunter's study. Stuffed birds, deer antlers and a shotgun were hanging on the walls. The dressmaker was sitting on the bed, half-naked, rocking rhythmically on top of a rag-filled dummy dressed in a man's suit.

Strawberry

SO WHERE'S THE YOUNG LADY GOING, ALL BY herself? Częstochowa? The train's really crawling along today, isn't it, just crawling along, but we'll be in Korwinów before you can say knife. Where are you from, miss? Hektary? My goodness. I used to live there myself. Do you know the birch grove by the forest? When I was a young lad, I used to go mushroom picking there, with Jadzia, the Nowaks' girl. Oh, Jadzia... she was pretty as a picture. You look a bit like her, young lady.

What was I saying? Ah, yes. Before the war, the place was full of mushrooms. They spread like wildfire under the young birches. You just had to take care not to mix up the good ones with the bad. We used to put salt on them and grill them on stove lids. I've never eaten anything better in my life. They tasted like heaven.

Oh no, in the countryside before the war, you'd never

think of buying toys for kids. We didn't even have a privy, only a bucket in the hallway. The girls played with dolls made from corncobs. Do you know, miss, how to make a doll like that? Before the corncobs ripen, they grow green and lilac silks, just like hair. Jadzia loved those cobs. I used to go behind the priest's field and bring back a few inside my shirt, so that she'd have some for later.

In July of thirty-nine, we would play in our little hollow almost every day. There was a stream running through it. The water was cold and shallow, but we wanted to swim, so we dragged together lots of sticks and stones. It was hard work for a couple of days, but when the dam was ready the water rose and made a little pond. We splashed around till evening, with burdock leaves on our heads to keep the sun off. When we got bored of splashing, we'd have a rest under the oak tree. That oak tree is still there, isn't it? Even the Germans didn't touch it. Ha! Jadzia loved lying under that oak, flushing the game from the clouds, as she'd say. Around five, we'd usually go home our separate ways. Hiding from everyone, Jadzia and I would sneak into Sitkowa's barn, go up to the top of the mow, which was full of hay, and slide down on sacks. I'd climb up to the very peak with a hat full of chaff and toss it out so that it rained down over the threshing floor. Jadzia had such fun with this, until a husk got into her eye and she started bawling and ran off home.

One day, I leaned down to scoop up some chaff into my hat, and my shirt rode up. Jadzia saw the birthmark on my back – a strawberry, we used to call it back then, miss. She started laughing and fled from the barn. I chased after her, but she'd hidden somewhere behind the woodshed, the little demon.

The next day, I made myself a bow out of a hazel branch, grabbed a hunk of bread with lard and went to look for the other children. I was surprised because they were already waiting for me by the road. I ran up to them to show off my bow.

'Witch child! Witch child!' they yelled at me.

I dropped my bow. They trampled it. The string snapped. They knocked me down, spat on me, pelted me with addled eggs and cowpats. I tried to break free, I tried to shield my face with my hands... Finally, I rolled into the ditch and ran off into a field. I hid in a storage clamp... At dusk, I heard Mother calling me. I came out of the clamp, rinsed my face in a wooden pail and ran home, swallowing fresh air, blood and tears. Mother was waiting in the hallway with a carbide lamp. I was such a fearful sight she crossed herself when she saw me, with my torn-up shirt and black eye.

Mother lit the stove, pulled out a wooden washtub from behind the curtain in the hallway and got a bath ready. The warm water calmed me down a bit. When the bath *had cooled, she pulled me out, wrapped me in a sheet and rubbed iodine into my wounds. I couldn't get to sleep. I tossed and turned in bed until morning. It all came back to me, those brats beating me by the road, and I thought I saw Jadzia among them. But I never breathed a word to anyone about what happened by that road.*

On the Feast of the Assumption, I picked hollyhocks, tiger lilies, whatever I could find by the fence in the garden, and I went over to the roadside cross. Rain was lashing down on the little shrine as I begged Our Lady, Jesus and all the saints to let that rain wash the strawberry off my back. But the strawberry remained. I rubbed it with the juice of greater celandine, the way Mother would cure my warts, but that didn't help either. The strawberry stayed where it was, exactly in the same spot, except the juice turned it into a reddish-brown map.

In thirty-nine, miss, the first day of school fell on the fourth of September. I really didn't want to go. I was afraid the other kids would remember my strawberry and would start tormenting me again. I stuffed myself full of unripe fruit and got stomach pains. Mother gave me a snifter of walnut liqueur and by the afternoon I felt a bit better, but I didn't have to go to school anyway. You know, miss, the war had broken out and I stayed home. The people in the village seemed restless; they kept looking inside their wells, pacing back and forth between their barns and their pigsties, checking cellar doors and storage clamps.

When Mother went out to see a neighbour, I couldn't resist. I left the house and went to Sitkowa's barn. I sat down on a tree stump and started whittling a stick with my penknife. All of a sudden, someone pushed the door ajar. I saw the corner of a percale pinny. It was Jadzia. She opened the box behind the thresher where she used to hide her corncob and straw dolls, bottle caps and pebbles. Delighted, I ran up to her.

'Hello, Jadzia!'

And you know what, miss, she didn't say a word to me; she was distant and cross. We sat down on the highest beam, right under the roof of the mow, and looked out at our little hollow through a knothole in one of the planks. A gust of cool wind from the forest startled some partridges into flight. The autumn was coming, but I was happy because Jadzia had come back.

'So, what's up, Satan's child?' she snarled suddenly.

I knew that she wasn't joking, that this wasn't my Jadzia any more, but just another brat from the village, a stranger. I pushed her as hard as I could. My God, she fell right on top of the chaff-cutter. She lay there in a pool of blood. I fled from the barn to the forest. The bells of St Anthony's began ringing.

You look pale, miss. A bit of water? I always carry

a bottle in my bag, to wash down my pills. You see, miss, before you could say knife we're already in Stradom. This is where I get off.

The Woman with a Dog

WHEN WE FINISHED CARTING BUNDLES OF RIPE poppy heads in from the field, my mother went to smoke a cigarette behind the house and fell asleep under the apple tree by the pond. When she woke up, she called me over. Chewing a mixture of fresh seeds from crimson, purple and grey poppies, I lay down beside her and watched the sky spin candyfloss out of the clouds.

Accompanied by starlings, the wind was whistling an off-key melody in the drainpipes, tugging at the plastic foil over the tomatoes, rocking the metal signs by the road that said 'Christmas trees sold here'. Something rustled in the reeds. A golden orfe jumped out of the pond. My mother started telling me her dream about an old classmate, Stella Dynus, and wondered anxiously whether she mightn't have mysteriously contracted the little Stella's sleepwalking illness and would soon start running around the fields, as Stella used to do, shouting across the limestone pits that the Germans were coming. It was a Russian-doll kind of a dream, in which my mother thought she was Stella, but Stella dreamt the dreams of someone else – the Kurzaks' five-year-old daughter. The Kurzak girl, they said in the village, had been executed by a German firing squad in 1943 in revenge for the Jędruś' assault on the Hitlerjugend centre near Myszków. She was buried behind the priest's field, in what later became part of a state-owned farm.

Stella was the only one in the class who didn't go to religion lessons and the other kids teased her a great deal because of it, but Mum admitted that she envied her because the girl stood out from the rest, with her distinguished manner and elegant clothes. Back then, all schoolgirls wore identical cross-back pinafores, white linen shirts and dark blue pleated skirts, but Stella always looked more stylish: she had a collar with a crocheted edge and patent leather shoes. My mother used to sit next to her in art class and borrow double-ended coloured pencils, which Stella got from her family in America, as well as foreign paints and a red ballpoint pen with a rotating multiplication table.

Just before Easter 1968, Stella started missing classes, or she'd turn up late, with dark rings under her eyes. Strange rumours circulated around the village. The Dynus' nearest neighbour described how the girl would come out of the house in the middle of the night and wander around the fields wearing only her nightie, shouting something about the Germans. According to Mum, someone from our village had to finish dreaming the abruptly interrupted dreams of the Kurzaks, and for some reason it had fallen to little Stella.

After Easter, Stella didn't come to school again, and my mother thought she'd gone down with chicken-pox, like everyone else, and would soon show up in class covered with zinc cream – but she never came back. Apparently her family moved abroad. My mother never heard anything more, neither about Stella Dynus nor about the Kurzaks' wartime tragedy.

One day in August, my mother and I were sitting together on an upturned wooden washtub in the yard, shelling beans. Construction workers were making a racket on the state-owned farm close by, digging foundations for a new building. Two large excavators were taking turns spewing out rich black soil onto the field of stubble and goosefoot. After a while, a dark blue Volkswagen pulled up next to the building site. The car's wheels dug themselves into the mud. An elegant, slim woman in a blue waterproof jacket and white jodhpurs got out, followed by a black-and-tan mutt.

My mother walked over to the fence and waved at me. 'Wiolka, come here, I have a feeling that the woman with the dog is Stella Dynus from my dream,' she said. 'My word, she's grown.'

The tall woman with chestnut hair tied in a ponytail was walking slowly towards the construction site, stumbling on clods of ploughed earth. She stopped beside the foreman, who was leaning against a caravan. As soon as he saw her, he instinctively wiped his cheek on his sleeve and straightened up a little. The woman reached into her handbag, showed him a tattered newspaper cutting, explained something and pointed at a spot on the stubble field, gesticulating vigorously. He didn't even glance at the paper. He continued leaning on the caravan and wiping his muddy wellies on the grass. The woman didn't want to leave; she stubbornly kept explaining something, but the foreman just pointed at his temple, rolled his eyes and walked off towards the field kitchen, since a break had just begun.

A gust of wind snatched her scrap of newspaper and lifted it up like a miniature kite. The dog chased after it, but the paper corkscrewed down and fell into a lime pit. Golden-brown hazel leaves rustled above our heads. Water rippled in the wooden pail by the drainpipe. A cool breeze rose. My mother put down the basket of bean pods and went inside to get a jumper. I remained by the fence, picking at a mouldering post and looking in the direction of the state-owned farm.

The woman lingered a while longer by the cement mixer and tried talking to an older worker in a woollen cap who had emerged out of a combination bus. But he didn't want to listen to her either and hid inside again. Eventually, she gave up and started walking back to her car. The black-and-tan mutt dug up a molehill, ran after a dry leaf and then joined his mistress.

The workers clustered around the field kitchen like a single exhausted organism, collecting their portions of beans in aluminium mess tins and glancing back at her as she walked away slowly, swinging her hips.

The wind puffed out her jacket and lifted it up like a bright blue lantern.

Sour Cherries

IT WAS THE THIRD SATURDAY IN JULY. MY GRAND-mother woke me at six in the morning. I didn't have the energy to get up because I was tired after all the work picking sour cherries the day before. Finally, I dragged myself out of bed, washed my face in cold water and rummaged around in the medicine cabinet for salicylic acid solution and a safety pin, to pull out a splinter that was stuck in my left palm. I didn't find anything, so I just sprayed my hand with deodorant. My grandmother was waiting in the front yard, yelling, 'C'mon, c'mon, or we're gonna miss the bus!'

I dressed quickly and ran out into the yard. After the rain, the air smelled of watermelon pulp. When we passed the gate, my grandmother paused by the milk churns and told me to check if the milkman hadn't left any co-op butter or cheese inside. Sadly, the churns were empty that morning. We trudged down the cobbled road, lugging two bucketfuls of sour cherries each, to the bus stop in the neighbouring village of Wojsławice.

The morning bus to Myszków was stuffed like a sausage. People squatted on the floor or perched on top of sacks or fruit baskets. Animals were making a din in their cages. Sauerkraut brine was leaking under the seats. I crouched down by our sour-cherry buckets and watched puppies dozing in a satchel next to fogged-up plastic bags filled with broad beans. The sleepy driver wasn't paying any attention to this zoo. He adjusted his hat and tried not to drive into the ditch as he dodged potholes and herds of cows shuffling along to their pastures.

On Saturdays, all the spots at the Myszków market were taken, but this didn't faze my grandmother. She went up to a bearded man who was entertaining passers-by with card tricks on a portable fishing chair.

'Lord be praised,' the man spoke first, as if he'd known my grandmother for years. She didn't reply; she just adjusted her kerchief and handed him two rolled-up hundred-złoty notes. The fellow folded the chair and gave up his place, just like that, then walked off towards Pułaski Street.

'How much are sour cherries going for today?' my grandmother barely had time to call after him.

'Today, seventy.'

I knew nothing about these market customs, so I walked off to the side and spent a while pressing my sore palm against a cool wall. A bit later, I went back to help my grandmother measure out sour cherries with a pint-sized mug.

All of a sudden, Piotr, my first love – no fewer than nine Saturdays spent dancing together at the disco – appeared from around the corner. He was accompanied by a woman in her forties, the spitting image of TV presenter Krystyna Loska. They paused next to a stall with leather highland slippers. I guessed right away that this was his mother, a well-known doctor, about whom he'd told me so much. I wanted to vanish into thin air, to hide inside a bucket of sour cherries.

Dear God, I thought, *please make me disappear and I promise I'll go to midnight Mass this Christmas. Never mind midnight Mass, I'll even go on a pilgrimage to Częstochowa, just please, don't let them walk down this aisle. They mustn't see me here, I'm begging you. Oh shit, they're coming!*

I smoothed down my messy hair and licked my lips. My tanned face was freckled, my shorts were dirty, and I was a sorry sight. I put my juice-stained hands in my pockets and tried to hide behind my grandmother's back. It was all in vain: Piotr caught sight of me anyway.

'Girl, what on earth, what's got into you?' my grand-mother scolded me. 'You've nearly crawled into my bucket! You seen a ghost or something? Sour cherries, ladies and gentlemen, get your sour cherries! Picked just yesterday, ripe and juicy sweet!'

Piotr was looking at me with surprise. I forced myself to smile and wave, but he didn't respond; he turned the other way. They walked off to the left and disappeared behind stalls. I knew I'd never see him again. I sat down on the grass and with a single slap killed a red spider mite which had been strolling along my arm.

I don't remember how much time passed, how many hard, sticky hours my grandmother and I measured out in pints of sour cherries. I felt more like myself again in the late afternoon, when both buckets were empty. People walked past us. Ice-cream cones dripped down onto sandals. Instinctively, I started sucking the aching spot on the inside of my hand. My grandmother packed up our bags and gave me a few banknotes.

'Why so glum? Go on, girl, buy yourself something, and there'll be enough for your disco too.'

She wrapped the rest of the money in a little pouch and hid it in a secret place somewhere in one of her seven skirts. We left our things with a flower seller we knew and made our way through the deserted square towards the centre of town, treading on candyfloss sticks and soggy strings left behind from wreaths of little bagels. Puddles of pickle brine glistened on the warm asphalt. We stopped by a small shack covered with white plywood. My grandmother bought us two *zapiekanka* pizza toasties. When she wasn't looking, I threw mine into a bin.

We went straight to the local department store, commonly known as 'the tin shed'. A throng of workers returning from the paper mill poured into Pułaski Street. Soda-water carts wheezed next to little squares. The queues in bakeries and butcher's shops grew longer.

I walked around 'the tin shed' feeling feverish, reading banners, staring at misshapen mannequins, passing shelves of tinned food and vinegar adorned with faded crêpe-paper flowers and aspen-bast cockerels, looking at Soviet watches – Poljots, Zimas, Vostoks – and porcelain figurines laid out on tulle in glass cases. The clock by the tills showed nearly five. The splinter under my skin, with its crimson halo, throbbed and oozed poison into a two-inch red streak.

The Phillumenist

COLLECTING MATCHBOX LABELS TURNED OUT TO BE a difficult hobby. Because how can you bring your razor-blade to bear, with the necessary precision, on the label of that matchbox calling to you from the table during a name-day party, when Uncle Janek, the happy owner of the box, isn't drunk enough yet for it to be pinched, and there are no more vodka bottles in the crate behind the curtain? Familial singing had not managed to put my uncle to sleep, and neither had my grandfather's stories about the Soviet tank that drove into Balwierka's yard instead of into Warsaw. He even stayed awake through all my father's monologues on subjects such as taking a 'friendship train' to Russia, the smuggling of jewellery, the use of sulphates in the preparation of stuffed animals. So I decided I'd have to resort to drastic measures. I scattered peppercorns on a hot baking tray. The smell of burning pepper had the same effect as tear gas: all the guests quickly evacuated to the yard, while I, with a kerchief over my face, could finally take care of the 'Storm' matches in peace.

In time, I learned to lift matchboxes from tables, wall units and dressers using knives and spoons, to work with fishing line and hooks or to simply wait until everyone had gone to do the chicken dance at a New Year's Eve ball. Eventually, however, my battles under the banner of the State Match Monopoly began to wear me out.

One day, when I sat down in the front row in maths class, I was suddenly struck dumb. A yellow 'Pomeranian Griffin' from Sianów – '64 matches for 25 groszy' – was lying on Mr Kropik's desk, tempting me ruthlessly. I had been hunting the Sianów griffin for a year, hoping that one of the long-distance lorry drivers who popped into the Jupiter for lunch would leave one behind, or that Natka Roszenko would bring one back from the Baboon Club – and now there it was, as luck would have it, belonging to none other than my maths teacher, who didn't like me because my surname reminded him of a soldier who had deserted from the Lubliniec army unit many years earlier. I never admitted to Mr Kropik that this unfortunate private was indeed my dad, but he suspected it anyway, and I had a feeling that he wanted to get back at me somehow but couldn't find an excuse. After all, I was an exemplary pupil and a scout; I went to every competition organised by the Polish Red Cross, the Voluntary Labour Corps, the Volunteer Fire Service, to vigils at the Tomb of the Unknown Soldier in Koziegłowy, to contests and workshops – in other words, wherever schoolchildren could get a free meal. At last, Mr Kropik caught me in the act of trying to appropriate his empty matchbox and with evident satisfaction sent me to the headmistress's office.

Luckily, I had a few old labels in my school bag that day because I wanted to show them at a meeting of the history club. I slowly laid out my collection on the headmistress's desk, presenting it as a learning aid. I pointed with my pencil to a 1920s 'Eastern borderlands' label and began describing how in 1925 the lower house of Parliament leased out the State Match Monopoly to a Swedish company headed by Ivar Kreuger, the 'Match King', in exchange for an unimaginable sum. Of course, I neglected to add that the government used the profits from this transaction to build the port of Gdynia, the pride of the unmentionable Second Polish Republic. The headmistress was very pleased with my explanations and wrote only a brief note to my parents.

A month later, my cousin from Lgota invited me to her wedding, and for lack of a better option she paired me up with the well-known local bachelor Romuś Lepiarz. He was around thirty. During the bridesmaids' and ushers' social evening before the wedding he was already coming on to me, and later, in a lorry on the way back from a trip to the forest to get conifer branches for the newlyweds' ceremonial gate, he even tried to put his arm around me, but I hid behind some spruce boughs.

On the day of the wedding, as custom demanded, I pinned a freesia and asparagus-fern boutonnière to Romuś's jacket, and in exchange he presented me with a box of chocolates and drove me to the church. I thought our joint duties would be over after the Mass and the ritual circumambulation of St Anthony's altar, but unfortunately that was just the beginning. I had to sit next to Romuś at the table and also dance with him. When during the 'my handkerchief' game Romuś threw down his snotty chequered nose rag in front of me, kneeled down and stuck out his gob for a kiss, I couldn't bear it any more and fled from the fire station. Fifteen minutes later, Mum made me go back to the hall and told me not to 'bring shame on us' and to endure Lepiarz's attentions until the end of the party. So Romuś continued pouring vodka for me and terrorising me in turn with creamy Swiss rolls, rollmops and devilled eggs. Mum's argument about 'not bringing shame' wouldn't have worked on me that night if it hadn't been for a certain small detail, imperceptible to others but highly significant to me: Romuś had a box of Orbis travel agency matches featuring Kraków's famous Lajkonik horseman, precisely the label I needed to complete a series. The problem was that he kept going outside to smoke, with the Lajkonik matches in his jacket pocket.

After a riveting game of cabbage-head football, which was won by the bridegroom's team, Romuś, sweating like a pig, wiped his forehead with his snotty chequered handkerchief, ate a chicken thigh, drank three rounds and went to the loo without his jacket. I was reaching into the inner pocket for his Lajkonik matchbox when he suddenly sprang out of nowhere right in front of me. Cold pigs' trotters quivered on a plate. Grapes fell into the sauce boat. Romuś grabbed my hand and squeezed it so tight that I almost passed out.

'We're leaving,' he hissed, pulling me towards the exit.

We stopped behind the fire station. I was so scared I grabbed hold of the lightning conductor, just in case. A flabby balloon was dangling over my head. My bun, which I had misted with hairspray, was slowly unravelling in the damp air.

'What are you gonna say now, you crafty little thief? You wanted to nick my wallet, eh?' He leaned down and I smelled the stench of half-digested vodka.

'No, not at all, I just wanted to see your Orbis matchbox label. I swear.'

'What? What label? Don't bullshit me. I'm not that drunk.'

'No, Romuś, honestly, I collect matchbox labels. Ask anyone.'

A long line of guests spilled out of the building, and one of Romuś's drunken friends started yelling at the top of his voice, 'A couple in love! A couple in love!' Romuś gave him a friendly wave.

'My car's over there.' He pointed at the maroon Fiat 126p by the fence. 'If you're not there in fifteen minutes, I'll tell everyone at the after-party tomorrow that you tried to nick my wallet.'

That was too much. I burst into the fire station to grab my handbag, announced to my parents that I had got food poisoning from the cabbage stew and, without waiting for their reply, ran past drunk Uncle Lolek, purple-permed Aunt Salomea and the waitresses carrying trays of steaming tripe. I headed for the back of the building, where I knew the firemen had a little storage room. I pushed aside helmets and dusty Volunteer Fire Service banners to get to the window, jumped out onto a manhole cover and ran straight home across a patch of beets in my high heels.

I left the muddy shoes in the hallway, lit the stove, pulled out my shoebox of labels from the cupboard and pushed apart the stove lids. I decided I had to put an end to these phillumenic games once and for all before they turned me into a nervous wreck. I threw the labels one by one into the fire and watched with strange satisfaction as they burned: the thirtieth anniversary of the Polish People's Republic, national censuses, anniversaries of the Volunteer Fire Service, Polish–Soviet friendship months, War on Tuberculosis days, adverts for Zefir king-size menthol cigarettes, Ruch newsagents, Presto fly killer, Wólczanka shirts and Marago coffee, collections of Polish fish, mushrooms and flowers ordered specially from the woman at the corner shop in Wojsławice. The smell of burnt cardboard and wood woke up my grandmother, who popped her head into the room. Seeing her, I calmed down a bit and put the remainder of the collection back in its shoebox. I lay down on the sofa in my crumpled dress next to the cat and fell asleep.

Dolce Vita

I HAND-WASHED THE ONLY JEANS I OWNED, A PAIR of Mawins which my father had bought for me from a pedlar, and hung them on the stovepipe to dry. Water dripped rhythmically from the trousers onto the floor, spreading into a blue puddle. I decided to take advantage of the fact that everybody had gone to Aunt Salomea's to celebrate her name day: I built a makeshift screen out of the chairs and the bedspread, poured water from the cauldron into a plastic tub and started to bathe. Steam scented with the fragrance of Familijny shampoo drifted up towards the soot-covered ceiling and condensed on the golden face of the Black Madonna.

I could hardly wait for the following day, when I'd cycle over to Natka Roszenko's house, which was famous throughout the whole region. Actually, it wasn't Natka's house; it belonged to Cynga, who – according to Natka – had gone for a few months to East Germany on business.

The next day after lunch, I announced to my mother that I was taking my bike to Natka's. She barred my way to the barn, where I kept my bicycle.

'You're not going! How shameful! Everyone in the village knows what an oddball she is.'

'I *am* going. You go there yourself on Sundays to buy cigarettes and Hungarian tops.'

There was silence. Taken aback, my mother let me pass.

'Fine, go ahead, if you're so grown-up – but don't come crying to me later!' she yelled after me angrily, shaking her fist.

I turned from our dirt drive onto the cobbled road, then onto the main road, where my bike chain kept falling off and I got covered in grease up to my elbows pulling it back on.

I stopped in front of a two-storey villa on the main street of Markowice. The façade, covered with broken mirror shards, was reflecting the afternoon sun, and the house looked like an enormous rippling aquarium.

'Come in, come in! I have new labels for you!' Natka shouted from the half-open window of the kitchen.

I wiped my grease-smeared arms on a cleaning rag drying on the radiator, took off my plimsolls in the hallway, entered the bright sitting room and sat down on a cream leather sofa. The walls were decorated with strange rugs and a picture of an angel dissolving in red and gold paint.

'That's Pryjma-Tamioła,' said Natka, emerging out of the kitchen dressed in black jeans, a studded belt and a red top, and smelling of tomato and basil spaghetti.

'Who?'

'That painting – it's by Roksolana Pryjma-Tamioła from Lviv.'

'Oh, cool. Where did you learn to cook like this?'

'I met an Italian guy at the Baboon who came many times to see me when Cynga wasn't home,' she laughed. 'This Italian showed me how to boil the pastas.'

Natka treated us to at least two bottles of Sophia wine. We were pretty sloshed when she leaned over to remove a speck of black olive from the corner of my mouth.

'I think I'm going to head home.'

'Why in such a hurry? You want to go pedalling that old machine at this time in the night? Why don't you stay to morning. We can watch videos.' Instead of replying, I burped loudly. 'Or maybe you want something else?' She opened the drinks cabinet, revealing fanciful bottles of alcohol and a pile of sweets.

'Go on, pick a box of chocolates, don't be shy.' She touched my hair and French-kissed me. I stood dumbstruck on the colourful mat.

'Your skin is dry. Come on, I show you how to fix it.'

Swaying, Natka led me to the bathroom. She staggered on the slippery floor.

'You find lavender oil on the shelf. Go on, have a bath, don't be shy. You have to rub it into damp skin.' She smiled and left the bathroom.

I looked around. Everything was sparkling clean. The walls were covered with cream tiles from floor to ceiling. I opened the wall cabinet. Apart from the indigo bottle of Pani Walewska, everything was unfamiliar: packages available only at a Pewex shop, with names like Dior and Lancôme. A perfume bottle labelled 'Dolce Vita' which looked like a crystal sugar bowl caught my attention. I sprayed my wrist. The scent of vanilla cupcakes and summer filled the room.

I took off my jeans without thinking and threw them on top of the washing machine. Drunk, I got into the bathtub – or rather fell into the water.

'I think I'm going to puke,' I muttered to myself.

'You called me, Wioluś?' I heard from behind the door of the bathroom. 'Can I come in? It's got cold in the house.'

I didn't reply. A moment later, Natka was sitting opposite me in the tub, naked. I felt her prickly, shaved groin against my thigh. In the water, the slender misproportioned body with small crimson nipples looked like a beetle with an elongated abdomen which I used to see sometimes by the edge of the pond but whose name I couldn't remember. It had two red spots on its wings. And that's when something struck me – a strange memory of a stormy day, visions of spiders jumping out from behind paintings. My head spun. Little ducks glued to the tiles turned into yellow gnomes and reached out their vile, wart-covered paws towards me. I jumped out of the bathtub like a scalded cat, threw on my clothes and ran out of the villa without saying goodbye.

Masters of Scrap

IN EARLY JUNE 1989, MY BREASTS GREW AND THE boys in my class began to tease me. One day, Older Lajboś sat down behind me in music and started snapping my bra. We were in the middle of playing 'The Girls from Opole' on glockenspiels. On *la*, I prayed for the stupid lesson to end at last; on *sol*, the mallet fell out of my hand and the pre-war tile stove in the classroom collapsed.

When I got home, I told my grandfather about the stove incident. Without saying a word, he went up to the wardrobe, poked in the keyhole with a piece of bent wire, opened the creaky door, took a little notebook out of a winter coat and put a cross in a chart next to the year 1934.

'That stove's given up the ghost, but it was first-class work. Show me another stove in Hektary that's lasted so long without asphyxiating anybody.'

My grandfather was a tile-stove builder, among other things, and he was recording the history of all the stoves he had ever built. In St Anthony's parish alone, he'd installed more than anyone could count.

That evening, he led me out into a field. 'You see the smoke from those chimneys?' He pointed with a dry stick. 'They're mine. I'm keeping an eye on them. In the evenings, I come and stand on the hill to watch how they're doing and see if the smoke is rising evenly up to the clouds.'

After the tile stove in our classroom collapsed, my grandfather's handiwork was carted off piece by piece in a wheelbarrow and dumped behind the rubbish bins. The next day, all the antique tiles had vanished, leaving yellow imprints in the grass. At school, work began on a central heating system and classes had to be combined. During one lunch break, the headmistress assembled all of us in front of the building and read out a report titled 'A Thousand Schools for the Thousand Years of the Polish State', which put even the caretaker to sleep. When she had finished, she ordered the chair of the student council to establish a Student Society for the Construction of Central Heating, with the aim of organising a collection of scrap metal by the end of the school year. Then she looked at her watch, turned on her heel and went back to her office.

A few days later, the chair of the student council divided us into three groups and announced that the team which collected the most scrap would get to go on a trip to Warsaw. I was assigned to Hektary, together with the Lajboś brothers, Big Witek and Justyna. For starters, each of us managed to drag in some metal junk from home. I carried off three bicycle frames and a mudguard from the shed belonging to Uncle Lolek, who did nothing all day apart from smoking his pipe, breeding coypus and training pigeons, but when it turned out that our scrap pile was the smallest, we held a secret meeting in our hideaway in a pile of breeze blocks and came up with plan B. We marked potential targets on a specially drawn-up map of Hektary. We began by exploring barns and attics and looking in every shed, shack and pit, then we widened our search to areas beyond the priest's field: Świnica, Kolonia, Sarnia and Boży Stok.

Even though the end of the school year was fast approaching, the quest for scrap absorbed us utterly. Our parents said we'd gone off our heads and they kept well clear of us. I dreamt about scrap at night: it beckoned to me from old German bunkers near Zendek, from within dugouts, storage clamps and the nearby yew reserve. I started noticing objects which had never before interested me in the least. Thresher wheels, anchor plates, screws, mudguards, old cables and pipes all drew me like a magnet. After a while, we completely lost our minds: we would wander around construction sites, limestone quarries, vacant buildings and state-owned farms, looking into every hole.

One night, we somehow managed to cross the Rzeniszanka between Świnica and Hektary with a few large pieces of sheet metal, which we hid in the reeds. Tired, soaked and with splinters under our nails, we were walking home slowly, leaving wet footprints on the cobbled road. All of a sudden, a Dobermann jumped out from the gate next to the headmistress's villa, reared up in front of us like the hound of the Baskervilles and clamped its teeth onto Younger Lajboś's trouser leg. I was afraid it would go for his throat next, so without thinking I tore a mouldered board out of the fence and hit the beast on its black rump. The dog leaped towards me, growled and showed its brown gums. Just at that moment, the porch light came on and the headmistress appeared in her full glory, in a pink dressing gown and slippers, with rollers in her hair.

'Trinket!' she yelled. 'Trinket, come here!'

The dog wagged its tail amiably, crawled back through a gap in the fence and scampered off into the yard. We breathed a sigh of relief. In recognition of my heroic deed, the boys gave me a badge carved out of bark and a huge sunflower head from the state-owned farm.

Two weeks passed. We met in our hideaway in the pile of breeze blocks. Big Witek stuck a Donald Duck bubblegum comic to his forehead and announced that we had less scrap than the Wojsławice team and that we'd have to go to Balwierka's house.

'Have you gone nuts?' said Justyna. 'That place is haunted.'

'It can't be haunted as long as she's alive. You're all just scaredy cats, that's all,' Big Witek declared.

'I'm willing to bet there's no scrap in that house,' Older Lajboś said.

'Okay, let's bet. If we find even ten pounds, you're going to jump into the septic tank.'

'Fine. Wiolka, cut the bet,' Older Lajboś said, turning to me.

To keep the peace, I brought my hand down like a blade over their handshake, and we left our hideaway among the breeze blocks.

At Balwierka's house, water dripped from the ceiling, drumming out a march in a rusty basin. Medicine bottles stood on a night table by the bed. The linoleum and the carpet runner stank of valerian, urine and lye.

'Hello. My grandmother Stefania sent me. Do you recognise me?' I asked. I sat down on the edge of the bed, stirring up clouds of dust, which got caught in a light beam and swirled around lazily. The old woman nodded. 'I've brought you something from Grandma.' I handed her a paper bag full of biscuits. Balwierka took it and started eating greedily. When the bag was empty, she licked out the remains of the icing sugar, turned to face the wall, which was adorned with a linen embroidery of a lake and pink flamingos, and fell asleep.

'Wiolka, what's wrong with her?' asked Younger Lajboś.

'I don't know. I think she's fallen asleep,' I answered sadly.

'Well, if she survived being invaded by a Soviet tank, she'll pull through just fine,' Older Lajboś quipped.

'Come on, let's take a look in the cellar. Maybe there's some scrap down there,' Big Witek whispered.

We pushed aside the trapdoor and went down the ladder one by one, but apart from two candlesticks, a crucifix and a leaky metal tub, we didn't find any scrap. Instead, Big Witek sniffed out a crate covered with hay which turned out to contain four bottles of homemade wine. Older Lajboś uncorked them with his penknife. We poured the wine out into glass jars. Bits of cork floated in the liquid, which was as thick as half-set jelly and tasted like musty blackcurrant juice. We sat down in a circle on the clay floor and started playing spin the bottle. Younger Lajboś spun first, and when the neck pointed at his brother we all burst out laughing. We carried on playing until midnight. I had never before had so many tongues in my mouth, and the next day I got a cold sore on my lip.

On Sunday, we didn't look for scrap. Towards the evening, we met in the birch grove, gathered a lot of dry branches and started making a campfire for a feast. We greased the inside of a cast-iron cauldron with lard and added layers of sliced potatoes, carrots, beets, onions, sausages, parsley, celery and leeks, then seasoned it all with bay leaves, salt and pepper and put young cabbage leaves on top. We placed the cauldron on a specially prepared brick hearth. Big Witek had brought a churn of soured milk from home, an indispensable drink to accompany our dish.

'Anyone got a piece of paper?' asked Older Lajboś, bending over the hearth.

'I'll pop over to Grandma's. She keeps issues of *The Sunday Visitor* under her straw mattress,' his brother shouted in reply, and soon he was back holding a magazine with Saint Faustina on the cover. Older Lajboś shoved a bit of dry grass under the sticks and lit the paper. Big Witek started laughing, saying we should thank Saint Faustina, because it usually took Older Lajboś a good quarter of an hour to start a fire. When the smells from the cauldron were strong enough to set all the dogs in Hektary drooling, the boys slipped wooden sticks through the handles, lifted the cauldron out of the fire and started serving purple portions of baked potatoes on rinsed burdock leaves.

After we finished eating, we cleaned the cauldron with sand. Older Lajboś insisted on walking me home, even though our field was only a stone's throw away from the birch grove. We set off towards the pond, stepping on young puffballs on the way. Smoke stung our eyes. We both smelled like *kabanos* sausages. Our hands met in the darkness. Older Lajboś stopped, looked at me peculiarly, wiped my sooty freckled cheek with his sleeve and handed me a little piece of cardboard. I looked at the gift and flung my arms around his neck. It was a matchbox label I had been after for ages, from the match factory in Czechowice: 'More scrap – more steel, 64 matches for 25 groszy'.

'Where is it?' he asked in a lowered voice.

'I'll be right back.'

I went up to the fence, groped in the dark for the gap between the mossy stone and the boards and pulled out a little jar of Butapren glue which I'd pinched that morning from my father's taxidermy toolbox. We sat down inside a reinforced-concrete well ring. Older Lajboś dribbled the honey-coloured gloop into a little plastic bag. We took turns sniffing it. In the thick, impenetrable silence, I heard the rhythmic throbbing of my blood.

Under the plastic, which billowed out and deflated like a white jellyfish, shoals of fish multiplied, tickling my nose and throat with their fins. I started giggling. I was lying under a waterproof jacket. Older Lajboś nestled his head between my breasts and began to caress me. When he slipped his hand inside my knickers, I tried to pull away, but he held me back gently. The little flowers printed on the cotton fabric grew moist. I looked up at the sky. The handle of the Plough was pulsating with a bright metallic glare in the biggest scrapyard in the universe. I shivered, parted my thighs, and just as I felt Older Lajboś's finger inside me, I heard my mother's voice from behind the hazel trees: 'Wiolka, time to come home! How many times do I have to call you?!'

After two weeks of collecting scrap, the five of us had become the terror of Hektary, Kolonia and Świnica. Anyone could suddenly find themselves missing a hinge off their gate, a chain, a key, an anchor plate; we were instruments of unexpected loss. Most of all, we loved wandering around makeshift rubbish tips which the locals had started in disused limestone quarries; we would disarm old lamps and radios with a hammer and blow up deodorant cans in campfires.

The last day of collection was nearly upon us when Older Lajboś announced that he'd secured so much scrap at his uncle's that we wouldn't be able to carry it:

we needed to borrow a cart from somewhere to get it over to the school. The next day, I got my grandfather to lend me the cart he used for transporting hay from the field to the barn. When we arrived, Older Lajboś's words were confirmed: it turned out that his uncle had a whole shed full of metal junk. We loaded it all onto the cart, drank a glass each of fresh milk straight from the cow and began slowly dragging our booty home.

Suddenly, the heavy cart, with its cargo of scrap tied on with pieces of rope, started rolling towards a precipice. We tried to stop it by pulling on the handle as hard as we could, but Younger Lajboś lost his grip, slid down along the wet grass and hung suspended over the chasm. With the last of his strength, he managed to grab on to something, I don't know what, maybe roots or brambles.

'Oh my God! Oh my God!' Justyna squealed. 'He's going to fall!'

'Don't look at him, just hold on!' yelled Older Lajboś. But then he also let go of the handle, threw himself down on the grass in front of where his brother was hanging and reached out his arm to rescue him.

'Put a stone under the wheel first! Fuck, do you hear me? A stone!' Big Witek shouted.

The cart was moving closer and closer to the edge. We couldn't hold on any longer. Older Lajboś managed to pull his brother up in the nick of time. Almost simultaneously, we all let go of the handle and jumped back. The cart tilted and slid down into a deep limestone pit filled with dark water. Our haul of scrap, our chance of top grades and a perfect conduct mark on the final report, our dream tickets to Warsaw all plunged with it into the abyss, but we weren't paying attention any more. We lay on the trampled grass like waterlogged fascines, sweaty, passive, with sore arms, but strangely calm.

'That's it for collecting scrap,' I said hoarsely.

'The headmistress can piss off with her contest,' Older Lajboś finished my thought. The others agreed.

I looked in the direction of the village. The smoke from my grandfather's stoves was rising straight up to the clouds. The low sun was rusting over the fields.

The Return of Zorro

ONCE IN A WHILE, WHEN MY MOTHER WENT TO visit her sister in Katowice, my father would invite his pals from the paper mill over for a little game of poker. I would sleep in the dining room, those evenings, with nothing better to do than eavesdrop on their conversations, since the men spun fantastic tales about silver foxes, fishing accessories, Rambo films and their adventures in the army. Only Tadek, a guy who had the look of a sacristan, usually just nodded in agreement and said nothing about himself.

Late one night, when they could hardly stay upright in their seats, I nodded off, and when I woke up well after midnight I could hear Tadek telling a story which made it clear that he was no sacristan at all, but a pickpocket with multiple convictions, well known throughout Europe. In 1973, his father had got into a drunken fight and gone to prison for three years. His mother earned a pittance working at a grocer's shop and could barely make ends meet. When Tadek turned thirteen, he decided to help her somehow: he started collecting cans and bottles left by pilgrims in Staszic Park near Jasna Góra. That's where he met a swindler from Lviv who taught him the trade, meaning he turned the boy into a petty thief. After Tadek filched his first wallet, he bought himself a pile of pastries at Blikle's. He also gave a Zorro costume, complete with a cape and a mask, to each of his friends from Krakowska Street. Vocational school was not young Tadzio's strong point, but he was a very diligent pupil of the Lviv swindler. He brought home more and more money, treated his mother to a leather handbag and a suit, and would tell everyone that he was earning extra cash working at a cobbler's – while in fact he and the Lviv swindler went marauding at train stations in Warsaw, Bratislava, Berlin and Vienna.

'Sometimes I managed to make twenty K in ten minutes,' Tadek finished, and I almost choked on a piece of halva.

My father knew Tadek well, so unlike me he let these stories go in one ear and out the other. That night, Dad wasn't having much luck with the cards. Every so often, he'd lose a game and would run to get more jars of pickles and preserved mushrooms from the hallway, stoke the fire in the stove or demonstrate his disappearing-coin trick to his friends, while trying to figure out a way of not being dealt in again.

I had worked out that coin trick of his only shortly before, when I learned that he had ordered a special one-złoty piece, with the reverse hollowed out, from a turner he knew in Cynków. Its diameter was slightly larger than that of a normal coin, so that when somebody put their złoty on the table, all that was needed was a dextrous movement of my father's hand for it to disappear for ever inside the magic coin.

Alas, pickled mushrooms, sardines, tinned snails and other delicacies could not save my father; neither could his burnt-match trick, which involved wrapping an invisible thread around the carbonised head of a match and breaking it off with one precise jerk. Play continued. When my father had nothing more left to lose, he promised his friends he'd taw them three muskrat skins each.

In the morning, after downing two glasses of water with baking soda and vinegar, my father tried to get ready for work: he ran around the room knocking over bottles, opening and closing wardrobe doors and getting tangled up in the leads sticking out from behind the wall unit.

'Oh my God, where's my wallet?! It was in my jacket pocket yesterday!' he yelled so loudly that the flypaper swayed under the ceiling lamps.

'Shh, Dad, or you're going to wake up Grandpa,' I said sleepily from the adjacent room. 'What do you need your wallet for anyway, now that you've gambled away all your pay?'

Silence fell.

'All of it? Oh, I'll make it up, I have some goshawks I can stuff. But right now I need to find my wallet because my monthly bus pass is in it.'

The problem of the lost bus pass seemed pretty serious to me. Even though I was sleepy and my head was crammed full of tales from the criminal underworld, like an issue of *Detective*, I could foresee what would happen in an hour, when Mum got back from her sister's in Katowice, saw the mess and caught my father at home, and in such a state to boot. I threw aside my duvet, drank some flat water straight from the soda siphon and went to help him with his search. We looked under the table and under the bed, in the wardrobe, among the crystal, in the coal scuttle. The wallet had disappeared off the face of the earth.

'Maybe you should say a prayer to Saint Anthony,' my grandfather piped up from his room, which took me by complete surprise, because for a long time I had thought he'd totally lost his grip. '"Dear Saint Anthony, please come around; something's been lost and cannot be found,"' he recited.

'Grandpa, how can Dad pray when he doesn't believe in the saints?'

'That's right, he only believes in his party. So he can pray to it, and maybe the party's going to give him back his wallet, and the pay he frittered away, and that house in Sosnowiec, and then he won't have to go to work any more.'

'Oh come on, just leave me be. Such harassment first thing in the morning…' my father replied. With resignation, he sank into a chair and laid his head on the table.

I had a sudden flash of inspiration. I went to look inside the glass hen where we stored eggs, and there, among cigarette ration cards, I saw my father's wallet. We checked its contents. Nothing was missing. A slip of paper fell out of his savings book to the floor: it bore the mark of Zorro. Before I could show it to my father, he grabbed his pass and ran off like a madman to the bus stop.

The Belated Feeding of Bees

ON SUNDAY RIGHT AFTER LUNCH, MY FATHER began preparing muskrat skins and cut his finger on a dirty penknife. An orange erythema appeared around the wound. When he got a fever, his lymph nodes swelled up and purple spots spread over his back, my mother called the ambulance from the village mayor's house. It came two hours later and took him away to the hospital, sirens blaring, with a suspected case of blood poisoning. My mother said they replaced all his blood and pumped medicines into his stomach with a special pump.

Miraculously, he managed to turn the corner after three weeks, but when he came home I hardly recognised him: he had lost more than twenty pounds and had gone almost completely deaf. His eyes had lost their brightness, and his formerly swarthy face had turned the colour of a horseradish root. He was given sick leave and for the time being stopped going to the paper mill. He would get up at seven, throw his camouflage jacket over his shoulders and look out of the dining-room window at the pond and the beehives, which stood scattered among bare currant bushes. At nine, he would wash, put on his loafers and change into a shirt and his favourite, slightly too-tight jumper with a black-and-white diamond pattern. After swallowing two raw eggs, he'd look through old illustrated books about birds and fish which he'd brought home from the recycling centre at the mill, or he'd take out an old hunting knife with a deer-hoof handle from his taxidermy box and would sit opening and closing it as if he were playing some sort of game. That's how it was almost every day: he didn't stuff animals any more, he didn't play poker, he didn't go fishing and, increasingly, he hardly ever said a word to anyone.

He perked up only when he read in *Beekeeping* magazine that over the course of the harsh winter the frost had destroyed numerous apiaries in southern Poland. He jumped up from the sofa, fetched a blackened saucepan from the dresser, poured in two bags of sugar, added hot water from the kettle and put the pan on the stove. About ten minutes later, the thick golden liquid began to boil, with bubbles of air escaping from the saucepan and touching my father's swollen fingers. The pleasant smell of caramel filled the smoky room. My father ran outside in his slippers, skidding on the icy path, and began installing feeders made from cut plastic bottles at the entrances to the hives, then filling them halfway with cooled syrup.

He returned an hour later and sat down resignedly on the sofa, which wobbled on its birch pegs.

'Damn it, I was too late,' he whispered miserably and shook the snow off his slipper onto the floor. 'I forgot to feed them in the autumn and all the colonies have died.'

For the first time in a long while, I had a chance to take a close look at him, and I noticed just how much he had aged in the past few weeks. He didn't blacken his moustache with the soot from the bottom of the kettle any more, and he looked as if he'd glued a rotten leaf under his nose. He had also stopped putting on a tie, and his snow-white shirts had started turning musty in the wardrobe. My searching gaze must have embarrassed him because he turned his face away towards the window.

I didn't know how to cheer him up. I felt sorry both for my father and for the bees, but I didn't let on. In those days, my teenage head was teeming with so many different thoughts at once that I preferred to keep quiet or, in secret from my mother, sneak up to the medicine cabinet and swallow more and more drops of Milocardin, which smelled of hops and mint. I took a Gdańsk Match Producers label out of my shoebox – 'Bees are your ally,

48 matches for 30 groszy' – and handed it to my father. Then I put on a jacket, moved to the unheated dining room and began studying German vocabulary for a test, taking advantage of my grandfather's absence, since the harsh jabber always irritated him.

An hour later, like twin comets, the tungsten filaments inside the bulb turned red, flickered and went out, but nobody in the house paid any attention. We were used to living in constant semi-darkness because of the fuses blowing, or the power station introducing energy-saving measures, or gale-force winds bringing down power lines. That evening, we sat in the glow of the stove like prehistoric insects frozen in amber: my father submerged in his new world of muffled sounds, and me stupefied by Milocardin and irregular forms of German verbs. The air shimmered over the hot stovepipe. Sparks shot out of the ash pan and vanished on the marbled lino like meteors falling into a dark, dense ocean.

My father looked pensively at the bee inscribed within a symmetrical sunflower on the matchbox label I'd given him, then he picked a leaf off the English ivy that was climbing along a fishing line between the lamp and the door frame and began playing such a piercing melody that shivers ran down my spine. Under the influence of my father's music, to which I was listening with pleasure for the first time, something woke up inside me and shook me out of my apathy. I smelled burning juniper branches, saw Gypsy caravans and people in colourful costumes jumping through flaming hoops in a forest clearing. My father stopped playing; he curled up on the sofa like a child and lay motionless. The shadow of a queen bee flickered in the window.

Unripe

THE SUMMER CAMP MANAGER DROPPED ME OFF by the main road. I waited until her rust-stained white Polonez disappeared in the fog behind the Jupiter Inn before crossing to the other side, stealthily wiping my tears. Next to a row of clay gnomes, I turned towards Hektary. I walked past the bus stop, the old women selling mushrooms and blueberries by the roadside, the holy spring, or rather a pit and a piece of mossy pipe, which were all that was left of it. The village, with its freshly asphalted roads and new signs – Long Street, Crystal Street, Green Street, Field Street – seemed foreign somehow, as if someone had tied it together with hair bands cut from the inner tubes of tyres.

I turned into our yard. A death notice pinned to the fence was blowing in the wind. A large white butterfly paused for a moment on the coffin lid propped against a wall. I was afraid to go inside. I sat down by the gate.

During the last two weeks of August, which I had spent at summer camp, the roof of the barn had had time to change colour from dirty green to brown.

Eventually, I went up onto the porch, laid my rucksack down next to the curtain in the hallway and smelled marjoram and melting wax. It was so quiet I could hear the pigeons cooing up in the attic. My grandfather was waiting for me in the kitchen with scissors and a little comb.

'You're here at last. Can you trim my hair?'

'Later, Grandpa. I don't have the energy right now.'

'But how can I show myself like this at the wake?'

'First I have to see how Mum is doing,' I cut him off and sat down on the edge of the bed, feeling tired.

'Oh. She's fine… I can cut my own nails, but hair? Just trim it a little at the back of my neck and around the ears, will you?'

'Okay, quick, give me the scissors.'

'Hurry up, before your mother comes.'

I flung a chequered tea towel over his shoulders and began cutting, slipping the comb under the hair the way my father had taught me and the way a pre-war barber had taught him when he was in prison. As I waved the scissors around all over the place, grey locks fell into the coal scuttle. My grandfather watched himself intently in a mirror to make sure I didn't cut off what he called the Danube wave over his forehead.

Pale and dressed in a black mourning outfit, my mother looked into the kitchen. It was clear she hadn't slept all night. I kissed her on the cheek to say hello.

'What are you two doing? Don't you have any shame? You're making a mess before the wake?'

'Shh, Zosia, I asked her myself. I can't go to the funeral all shaggy,' my grandfather replied.

'They were supposed to bring you home yesterday, not just in time for the wake,' my mother said to me coldly and passed me the Milocardin. I took a swig straight out of the bottle.

'It's a long way from Masuria. They didn't want to drive me back right away.'

'You could've called our neighbour from somewhere on the road.'

'I didn't have any cash for phone tokens.'

'There's sour rye soup on the stove. Do you want some?'

'I'm not hungry.'

'I'll serve you some because it won't be possible later.'

When I finished cutting my grandfather's hair, I washed my hands and went into the next room. The doors to the dining room were closed. My mother was arranging chairs in a row along the wall. On the window-sill, I noticed a blessed candle, a prayer book, a rosary and cakes laid out on stands covered with napkins. I grabbed a piece of chocolate cake and started helping my mother with the chairs.

'Don't you try to suck up to me now,' she said, smiling slightly.

I looked around the room. Everything was in its place: the porcelain tableware set, which served only as decoration and for keeping buttons and screws in its chipped sugar bowl, the glass hen for storing eggs, the glass fish, the stoneware knick-knacks, the barometer in the shape of a Tatra mountain cabin with the high-land woman looking out to indicate rain and the man emerging to forecast sunshine, the cockerels made from strips of aspen bast, the books which my father had rescued from the recycling centre at the paper mill in Myszków, the collection of empty beer cans crowning the wall unit. The stain on the ceiling, which used to be shaped like the pond behind our house, had swelled and become a river, its deltas running down the wall, feeding a network of fungus under the floor.

It struck me that our house was a kind of stone pro-sectorium, a cold store watched over by the bloodshot eyes of the stove, where I had grown as used to the fetor of decomposing animal flesh as I had to the sweet scent of bread. A wooden cross hung over the door, but some-thing else was the true religion here: the most holy books of zoology, the bird and fish guidebooks anointed with alum and dried Butapren glue, the eviscerated jackets with their padding removed, waiting faithfully at the bottom of the wardrobe for the master of ceremonies to return from the paper mill in the afternoon, spread out newspapers on the table and begin his ritual of taxidermy.

Mum handed me a mug of hot soup. 'Drink it down fast and go into the dining room.' She opened the double doors slightly and pushed me forward. 'You must.'

I burned my lips with the soup and paused on the threshold. The coffin lay on the table. It was handsomely made, varnished, surrounded by wreaths.

My father in a coffin? Was it really him? Maybe it wasn't, maybe it was just a stuffed double. A drop of dried wax on his lapel looked like a sliver of a yellow fingernail. A fly sat on the lace bolster.

'Get out of here, you vile thing,' my mother whispered, 'and don't you start breeding. I'll go and check, maybe there's a fly swatter in the dresser.' She left.

I sat down in the chair beside the coffin and touched my father's icy hand.

I saw an eight-year-old boy. He had skipped school again; he had hidden in a field of wheat. Brushing his curly hair off his forehead, he pulled a pâté sandwich wrapped in brown paper out of his satchel, but instead of eating it, he threw crumbs to the partridges wandering around in the wheat. He raised his head, looked straight at the sun, then squeezed his eyelids tightly shut, and in the flickering spots he saw the face of his mummy, who had recently died in Sosnowiec. They said the flu had weakened her heart. The inscription on the dark granite slab read, 'Sabina Rogala, née Szydło'; there was a star and a row of numbers, and then a cross and a row of numbers. He remembered her black plait and the way she sliced bread, holding the loaf against her breasts. A partridge came closer. Rysiu carefully took off his jacket and flung it over the wheat. A moment later, he was holding the bird, which flailed about under the fabric like a puppet.

Everything changed after his mother's death. Rysiu wasn't a little boy any more; he knew that his daddy, who was a policeman, wouldn't come home at night. Rysiu could peel an apple all by himself and eat it, and then the peels too, and when the peels were gone, he'd suck on a lump of sugar or make little balls out of oat flakes. The following day, the woman from next door came and gave Rysiu a slice of bread with lard. After her came a different woman, with a briefcase. She took him by bus to where his mother's parents, the Szydłos, lived: out in the country-side next to a forest, in a wooden cottage with a tar-paper roof. The windows in that cottage were so small. Red fab-ric casings stuffed with musty feathers poked out of the duvet covers, and when Rysiu went down with measles, he slept with his duvet uncovered because his grandmother said that the colour red would draw out the fever. At night, Rysiu was afraid; he kept calling for Mummy and had to sleep on the windowsill under a horse blanket and fresh walnut leaves, so that bedbugs wouldn't bother him. After Christmas, his grandfather pulled out a sheepskin coat from the shed. Rysiu didn't want to wear it to school, but Grandpa insisted.

'Hey, shaggy beast!' children yelled, throwing snowballs at him.

Spring came. Grandpa Szydło whitewashed the walls. Bedbugs stopped being a bother, and the children at school didn't beat Rysiu up any more, because he could draw so nicely that some of them even took his sketches of animals home and asked for more. On Sundays, he'd go to the forest with Grandpa. They would cut notches in pine trunks, collect the sap into a tin cup, set hare snares. Grandpa carved little bark boats for Rysiu, and they'd go to sail them together on Green Lake. Grandpa Szydło was probably the wisest man in the whole world: he could talk to animals and knew which mushrooms were good to eat and which were poisonous. They would bake potatoes together in the fire.

One day, Grandpa showed him a pine marten's nest in the hollow of a tree. Rysiu put his hand inside and groped around in the down until he felt the warm litter. He wanted to swap lives with the young martens, to come and live in the forest and share their bird eggs and rabbit holes – but he ran after Grandpa, because it got dark, and then afterwards he always had to run after someone and everything flew by like in an American film. There was never enough time or money. Rysiu kept rushing around, to earn enough for a new pair of shoes, for his first suit, to make it through his spell in the army, to buy himself a motorbike, to take Zosia to a dance, to be on time for the exam at the agricultural college, and for his wedding, and christenings, and for the night shift.

*

Twenty years passed. We were together on the bus to Myszków: my father was going to the paper mill and I needed to get a book for school. Dad was dozing in a seat at the back. He had turned up his jacket collar because the early morning was cold.

'What a strange world this is,' he said to me suddenly when the bus turned into Pułaski Street. 'Before I've even had time to blink, they're already calling me old, when inside I'm like an unripe fruit.'

One Sunday morning in late August, he took his bicycle and went fishing. He laid out his rods on the edge of Green Lake. He kept falling asleep and waking up because his left arm was going strangely numb and there was a burning in his chest. The bright-coloured float, which he had carved out of polyfoam, bobbed up and down in the water, but nobody was watching it any more. Before noon came, before the first tench swallowed the bait, this fifty-year-old boy was dead.

Neon over the Jupiter

A STRANGE SOUND RESEMBLING THE COOING OF a collared dove woke me up before dawn. I opened my eyes and heard the cooing again. I threw off my duvet, pushed the window ajar and looked outside. Older Lajboś was sitting on the broken apple-tree stump by the pond, in a halo of glow-worms.

'What are you doing here?' I asked sleepily.

'I'm getting out of Hektary. You coming with me?'

'Where to?' I did up a button of my flannel pyjamas.

'My old man got a job at a mine, so we're moving to a housing estate on Saturday.'

Slowly, I started waking up properly. I was cross that Older Lajboś had got me up so early, just when I had been dreaming my favourite dream about the outdoor painting workshop which I had attended a few years earlier. A white moth with grey spots was dragging itself along the fogged-up windowpane. It seemed particularly anaemic, so I finished it off with a slipper. I put on my jeans and a jacket, threw a couple of boxes of crackers into my rucksack and jumped out of the window into a clump of nettles. I sat down beside Older Lajboś on the stump.

'You've been huffing again?'

'I–I–I got pissed off at my folks,' he stammered out. He drew closer and tried to put his arm around me, but I got up.

'I can't sit on this thing for long or I'll get a bladder infection, so keep it short. Where are we running away to?'

'I've saved up some cash from returning bottles. We'll go to Częstochowa, to my aunt Jadzia's place, and then we'll see. Maybe to Central Station in Warsaw?'

'You're lucky, you know, that Mum forgot to let Bear off his chain last night, or he would've really fucked you up. If we're going, let's go.'

We walked in silence towards Świnica, beyond which the road, worn by long-distance lorries, twisted and turned; we walked slowly, like one walks after midnight Mass, like my father coming home on Sunday from a fishing trip or from a little game of poker, like the curate after administering extreme unction, like my grandmother returning from the fields dragging a pram, in which instead of her first-born, prematurely dead daughter,

there lay a bunch of ripe poppy heads covered with a
kerchief; we trudged on, full of doubts, through beet
patches, through pale blue rows of cabbages, through
fields of grain with hidden beds of poppies; we trampled
the grey heads of dandelion clocks. Brambles slashed
our legs. Warble flies bit us. We forced our way through
thickets, through burdock, sweet flag, rye fields encrusted
with cornflowers; we walked in a frenzy, stumbling on
crooked stakes in the ground, on limestone rocks, on
piles of steaming hay. Our trainers and trouser legs got
drenched from the dew, but we kept going, along the
field margin by the little hollow with an oak tree, where a
stream once ran and where before the war Jadzia Nowak
used to meet her teenage murderer with a strawberry on
his back. We walked through barren sunflower fields, once
weeded as part of community action projects by women
brought in a combination bus on Sundays; we walked
through pesticide-filled havens for birds and grimy children which Gienek the Combine Driver traversed every
day on his way back from the Jupiter.

'When it clears up, we'll catch the bus,' Older Lajboś
murmured under his breath, but I wasn't listening to
him. I walked with my shoulders hunched, trying to
think only about not stepping into a cowpat or a trap.
The sun began to look more and more boldly at its
reflection in the surface of clay-pit pools, ponds, flooded

quarries. Every now and then, I stopped to nibble on some crackers from my rucksack. Older Lajboś didn't want to eat anything; he just kept putting the little glue bag up to his mouth more and more often.

At last, we reached the bus stop. Older Lajboś lay down on the bench in the shelter and put his head on his rucksack.

'I gotta have a little kip right now because I have the shakes. Wake me up when the bus to Częstochowa comes. Okay?' He looked at me with bloodshot eyes. I nodded and started reading out to him the graffiti on the bus shelter: 'I love Kasia', 'Fuck Legia Warsaw', 'Your winter, our spring, Moominsummer'. Flies clustered on a half-dried turd covered with shreds of newspaper. I went behind the shelter and, because I was hungry, I started sucking on the sweet spikes of clover flowers. The bus to Częstochowa came, but I didn't flag it down. I gazed with apathy at the fields, the road, the dolomite quarry.

Across the street, two men in high-vis jackets were rolling a tractor tyre that had gone flat. An indigo neon sign lit up over the Jupiter. I suddenly thought of my mother, who since my father's death always got up at this time, with this neon sign, put on her mourning clothes with a housecoat over the top, brewed herself a cup of milky grain coffee, looked in on my ill grandfather and then came into the dining room, which I had converted into my bedroom and where I slept on the sofa under *Jesus Teaching from a Boat*.

'Get up for school, it's seven,' she'd whisper, put a mug of weak tea on the night table and pull off my duvet. What if this time, instead of me, she found three neatly arranged pillows in the sheets? Would she slump down dejected into the chair by the door, next to my posters of Republika and Perfect, or run out of the house to look for me on the road?

I glanced at Older Lajboś. He was breathing heavily. His pale spotty face looked like a badly risen loaf of bread. He was drooling. The little glue bag was sticking out of his pocket like a used condom. I couldn't stay with him at the bus stop any longer. I tied my messy hair with the rubber band which I'd cut from an inner tube and always carried in my jacket pocket, took off my soaked trainers and ran barefoot back to Hektary.

Translator's Note

WIOLETTA GREG'S DEBUT NOVEL IS SET IN THE Jurassic Uplands of southern Poland, in and around the small fictional village of Hektary, in the 1970s and 1980s. A brief explanation of some of the political and economic context of the period is provided here, especially for readers for whom the fall of communism in Eastern Europe is a historical fact rather than a memory.

The 1980s were the last decade of the Polish People's Republic, a communist-run state within the Soviet Union's sphere of influence. At the beginning of the chapter titled 'The Little Paint Girl', the narrator alludes to a moment which defined the era for a whole generation of young Poles. On Sunday 13 December 1981, children all over the country were waiting for that week's episode of the popular television programme *Teleranek* (which I have translated as *Telemorning*). The show never aired. Instead, General Wojciech Jaruzelski, the leader of the Polish communist government, appeared, dressed in his military uniform, and gravely read out a statement announcing the imposition of martial law – or 'state of war', as it is referred to in Polish.

This drastic measure was largely an attempt to crack down on the political opposition, which had emerged during a wave of strikes in the summer of 1980 in the form of the Solidarity movement, led by shipyard electrician Lech Wałęsa. A failing economy and frustration with decades of communist rule had combined to create a powerful challenge to the authority of the government. By late 1981, the one-party state was on the verge of collapse, and a so-called Military Council of National Salvation, headed by Jaruzelski, seized power. With martial law came arrests, military control of key services and industries, the banning of various organisations, renewed censorship and a curfew. Solidarity went underground, but the movement remained a popular force for change.

Life in the village of Hektary is punctuated more by folk traditions and the Church calendar than by political events, but historical developments are taking place in the background, from Lech Wałęsa's Nobel Peace Prize to Pope John Paul II's morale-building visit to his homeland in June 1983 (during which he met with both Jaruzelski and Wałęsa). The uneasy relationship between the Roman Catholic Church and the communist state is evident in 'Waiting for the Popemobile', when men from the village go to put up pennants by the roadside to welcome the Pope, only to encounter another group already waiting to destroy the decorations.

There are other ways in which the world of Hektary reflects the realities of daily life in Poland in the late communist era, with its scarcity of consumer goods and its flourishing black-market economy. The Polish *złoty* was virtually worthless abroad, circulation of foreign currency within the country was severely restricted, and ordinary shops frequently ran out of even basic necessities. Luxuries such as Natka's perfumes and the fabric for Wiolka's special dress could be bought on the black market or from Pewex, a chain of 'internal export' shops which stocked Western and Polish 'export-quality' goods available to purchase only with American dollars or with vouchers issued by the state bank. These vouchers, which were valued in dollars, could be obtained from the bank in exchange for foreign currency, as part of a complex and paradoxical system under which the use of dollars, Deutschmarks and other hard currencies was both forbidden and widespread. The ability to shop at Pewex, which implied some combination of money and social connections, was not necessarily to be flaunted. During times of scarcity and rationing, ordinary shops were often so poorly stocked that even the rumour of a delivery could trigger the formation of a long queue. Wiolka's mother claims that her sister queued all day to buy the fabric for Wiolka's dress, but the dressmaker can tell at a glance that it comes from Pewex.

By the end of the book, the 1990s are beginning and the communist era is over. The Soviet Bloc is collapsing and Poland is in transition, having held its first multi-party elections in June 1989. Yet while the book mentions certain developments in Hektary, such as the arrival of paved roads, the changes which Wiolka experiences – and the new maturity she develops – are intensely personal.

The theme of growing up is reflected in the book's Polish title, *Guguły*, which means 'unripe fruit'. This word also appears in two chapters. The narrator of 'Strawberry' recounts how he did not want to go back to school in September 1939, so he made himself ill by eating *guguły*. 'Guguły' is also the title of the second-to-last chapter, where I have translated it as 'unripe'. Near the end of this chapter, Wiolka's father tells her one morning – out of the blue, as their bus pulls into Myszków – that although in the eyes of the world he may already seem old, inside he is still like an unripe fruit.

ENGLISH PEN

FREEDOM
TO **WRITE**
FREEDOM
TO **READ**

This book has been selected to receive financial assistance
from English PEN's Writers in Translation programme
supported by Arts Council England. English PEN exists to
promote literature and its understanding, uphold writers'
freedoms around the world, campaign against the persecution and imprisonment of writers for stating their views,
and promote the friendly co-operation of writers and free
exchange of ideas.

Each year, a dedicated committee of professionals selects
books that are translated into English from a wide variety
of foreign languages. We award grants to UK publishers to
help translate, promote, market and champion these titles.
Our aim is to celebrate books of outstanding literary quality,
which have a clear link to the PEN charter and promote free
speech and intercultural understanding.

In 2011, Writers in Translation's outstanding work and
contribution to diversity in the UK literary scene was recognised by Arts Council England. English PEN was awarded a
threefold increase in funding to develop its support for world
writing in translation.

www.englishpen.org